FLORIDA ADVENTURE SERIES
BOOK ONE

Marco
AND THE FOUNTAIN
OF YOUTH

—

By Sam Payne

Illustrated by Kristopher Gillespie

AMERICAN ADVENTURE COLLECTION

Published by
American Legacy Publishing
1922 West 200 North
Lindon, Ut. 84042

Educators and librarians, for a variety of teaching tools, visit us at:
www.americanadventurecollection.com

Printed in China, March 2008

Quest for Magic Waters ...

"...Juan Ponce prepares to go away. But there is more."

"More?"

"You will laugh," said Alonso, "because you are already young."

"Already? You mean 'still young,' not 'already young,' I think," corrected Marco.

"Maybe," Alonso shrugged. "But word has reached Spain of a singular place of water—natives in the New World speak of it—a place of water in which an old man can bathe and become forever young and strong. Some say Juan Ponce will find it."

Marco laughed. "A good tale," he said.

Alonso shrugged again. "I told you that you would laugh," he said, "because you are already young." Alonso was silent again, and looked out to sea. For the first time since Marco had known him, his face seemed old and sad...

Book One in the Florida Adventure Series
from American Legacy Publishing

Chapter 1

Gray and enormous, the ocean spread from the docks at Càdiz, Spain. Among the dull buildings along the wharf, Marco sat in a shadow where two mossy walls made a dank corner. His dark hair hung loosely before his eyes. His bony arms were folded across his ribs. From here, Marco could see what anyone else on the wharf could see—like anyone else, he could see the *mercados*. To him, they stank of fish, and rang with the din of the shouting foremen—barking orders as nets and kegs emptied themselves among the wooden tables. Marco could see the gulls. The clumsy birds flapped in noisy circles overhead, screaming for scraps of fish or bread.

But Marco's dark eyes looked—and looked alone—for something he could not see. They did it without thinking anymore—even though his mind, without telling him, had found new tricks to keep from dwelling on the lost sailor. As Marco watched, the sea gnawed at the rocks along the shore. It sent up shocks of freezing spray as the waves rushed in on the wharf. Marco knew that out among the peaks and valleys of the dark waves, the sea swallowed men up. The fear of it sat like a stone in his stomach. And for two long years he had come each afternoon to this corner— to peer out over the water for his father.

"Marco!"

Marco did not turn or get up, but he waved his hand without thinking about it.

"Marco! *Vago!*" The voice came again. This time Marco turned to look. A grinning boy came toward him through the traffic.

"Vago? You call me lazy? You stink like fish, Pollito."

Pollito grabbed Marco by the hair. "And you," he said, "stink like two-year-old dirt." Pollito was ten—Marco's age, but a head shorter. His hair stuck out in all directions. His sharp nose pointed at Marco like an arrow. Marco liked Pollito. They were friends.

Marco pulled his head away. "My clothes are fine."

Pollito snickered. "Your father would kill you if he saw you like this." Marco bristled, but didn't say anything. Still sitting in the dirt, he looked up at Pollito. His friend was smiling, but his eyes were full of pity. Marco hated it when Pollito looked that way. He looked down again.

"Come on," said Pollito.

"You go. I'm busy."

"Oh yes, very busy. Get up." Pollito grabbed Marco by the hand and pulled him to his feet.

Pollito walked ahead of Marco with long paces. Marco followed with a lazy gait. They passed table after table. Impatient women bargained loudly with stubborn merchants. The sharp whack of a blade on a board sent a fish's head skittering into the street in front of Marco. He looked at it for a moment, then kicked it under a table.

The boys walked toward a fat man who stood behind a row of barrels. The man grinned to see Pollito. "Good morning, boy!" he said. He held his arms out and laughed.

"I delivered the milk, Señor Galdame." Said Pollito.

"*Bien, niño.* You do a good job, yes?" said Galdame. He wiped his hands on the large apron around his big waist. With one big hand, he patted Pollito on the head. With the other, he reached into a box of coins. Pollito kept looking at Marco. When Señor Galdame handed the coin to Pollito, Pollito held it up for Marco to see.

"There, now," said Señor Galdame. He chuckled. "Go and buy some bread—but come back tomorrow, niño. There is more work—like yesterday, like tomorrow. Always more work." Pollito thanked the man, and he and Marco began to walk away.

"And my saludos to your family!" shouted the fat man.

Pollito turned. "My greetings to yours also!" he waved back. Marco didn't turn, and didn't say anything.

As the boys walked, Pollito held out his empty hand as if it were one pan in a scale. "See, Marco," he said, "we do the work," he held up the hand with the coin in it, "and we get the money." He repeated the action, so Marco could see it again.

"Get off," said Marco. "You may get the money, but you have to get that stupid pat on the head from Galdame's fat hand." He shoved Pollito so hard that Pollito fumbled for the coin.

"Ow!" stuttered Pollito. "Listen, I'm only trying to say that if you'd work—"

"I eat, don't I?" interrupted Marco. His voice was sharp enough that a merchant and his customer stopped talking and turned.

Pollito fought back, his voice raised. "For two years you argue with gulls over alley scraps. Should your father come home today, he would be ashamed!"

"Leave me alone!" shouted Marco. He spun on his heel and marched off through the *mercado*. Behind him, he thought he heard Pollito call out, "Marco!" But his friend's cry had already been swallowed up in the smells and the shouts and the heat of the afternoon.

If Pollito followed him, Marco didn't look back to see it. Soon, he was alone—all alone, even though people walked in crowds all around him. He was alone, even though women and fishmongers argued as he passed. Surrounded by people—and yet all by himself. Marco walked quickly because he was still angry. "Pollito doesn't know anything," said Marco to himself. Pollito's father was a chandler. He bent over vats of wax all day every day, and never looked out at the sea. He was always in his home when Pollito left in the morning, and he was there when Pollito returned at night. What could Pollito know about losing a father to the wide ocean? Pollito's mother was the wife of a chandler. She was fat and kind, and even now argued over the price of bread with some *panadero* in this very *mercado*. Soon, she would cook dinner in the glow of her husband's candles. What did Pollito know of watching a mother's face covered in the cold sweat of a high fever?

What did Pollito know of watching parents die?

Marco's angry walk had taken him into the city—up and away from the *mercados* on the wharf. The houses were closer together here—the streets narrower. Deep alleys yawned on his left, and on his right. It was dusk, and the alleys were filling with dark shadows. The air grew cooler, but Marco's rage kept his face hot, and his muscles moving. What did anyone know of his grief? Both parents gone, and all Pollito could do was remind him how lazy he was. Lazy? Marco was dying inside! Pollito was a fool. How dare he! How dare he.

Marco's steps faltered as he rolled his ankle on a stone in the road. He bent down and picked up the stone. With a great yell, he threw it as hard as he could down a dark alley. He heard it ricochet off the side of a building. He heard chips of stucco fall to the ground. He heard the stone drop to the floor of the alley and skip across the alley dirt. Then all was still. Marco's chest rose and fell—his heart pounded. But he was no longer running away. For a moment he stood. Then, more slowly than before, he began walking again. He descended down toward the ocean—but away from the *mercados*. The path led him through neighborhoods, toward a beach one valley removed from the wharf.

Marco slowed, the angry energy going out of his stride

as he got further and further from the wharf. He was hungry, and it was getting dark. He stole into the space between two houses. Below the window was a small heap of rinds, peels, and cast-off greens. Marco reached out to pick through the food. As he did, Pollito's voice rose in Marco's imagination: "For two years you have argued with gulls over alley scraps!" it said.

He turned away from the pile. Tonight he could go hungry. He huddled against the alley wall. He drew his knees up to his chest and wrapped his thin arms around them. It was quiet in the alley—comfortable even. Marco closed his eyes. As he did, he heard a sound—air blown noisily through closed lips—like the noise a horse makes. Marco's heart leapt to his throat. His eyes opened wide. He scrambled to his feet and wheeled around. It wasn't a horse that had made the sound. A large man lolled in the alley. His clothes hung loosely about him in the dark. His mouth was wide open, and the smell of rum hung about him like a cloud. A few paces away lay another, smaller man. He slept like his fellow. Marco felt foolish for starting so. He took a deep breath to slow his heart. Sleep had been driven cleanly from his head. He sat down at the mouth of the alley. Marco didn't mind sharing the place. With his back to the two sleepers, he watched the sky slip from gray to black.

It hadn't been fair, he thought, to shout at Pollito. Marco had been set on edge, surely, by an afternoon of jibes about fathers and family. He knew Pollito was his friend. There was a soft, straw bed in Pollito's house that Marco slept on more often than anyone else did. Tonight, in the alley, Marco found himself longing for it.

But Pollito's words still smarted. He didn't want to work for Señor Galdame or for anyone else. He just wanted his father to come back to port. That's all he wanted—all he wanted in the whole world. But there had been no father for two years. No father and no family. Only Pollito, and bad dreams. Here in the alley, he thought clearly about it. It was Pollito who watched after him. Marco would never say it—least of all to Pollito—but the boy served as a sort of awkward guardian to Marco in his grief. The grief had dulled some, but never Pollito's playful care.

The last light left the sky. Night came on suddenly, and with it a chill in the air. Marco drew his arms tighter around his knees. His friend's words worked even further into his brain—past the place where they hurt, and into another place. He had not pride enough to work, he thought, so why did he have pride enough to stay angry with Pollito? It made no sense, and Marco knew it. In a rush of resolve he stood up, as a prelude to walking to Pollito's house for what Marco figured would be an awkward apology. The stars had begun to appear in the night sky. In the distance, the sea rolled out black from the wharf. The merchants had mostly gone home, and the stragglers were dimming their lamps one by one. Marco stood still for a moment, breathing.

Marco did not anticipate the urgent, whispered sound behind him: voices, in a language that Marco did not understand. Marco's breath caught in his throat, and he tried to turn, as a thick, dark sack came down hard over his head. Strong arms, quick as cobras, wrapped like great cords around his chest.

"*Què Diablos ... !*" shouted the boy. They were the last words he remembered. A sharp pain in his head, then the world faded in a cloud that reeked of rum.

——

Marco had a headache. That was the first thing he knew. The pain seemed to roll behind his forehead even before his brain came awake. He was on the ground. That was the second thing he knew. Voices were talking somewhere above him. He couldn't understand the words. A few seconds of talk, and then laughter. Then talk. Then laughter. Five or six people, he guessed. He lay there with his eyes closed, getting the feel of his body again. He began to feel sick—nauseous. The nausea came in waves, a few seconds apart. Marco wondered if he'd throw up. Slowly, he cracked his eyelids open. But between closing his eyes and opening them there was no change. Dark as night. Marco blinked. A few feet in front of him, a patch of dim light began to focus itself on the ground.

Marco pushed himself up on his elbows, and then to his hands and knees. He could feel the blood pounding through his head as he did it. He peered through the darkness at the light on the ground ahead of him. It was square—about the size of Marco's head. Maybe bigger—the size of his two feet held together. He tried to crawl toward the light. His head hurt. The nausea continued. His muscles ached. But he could crawl without much trouble. If he didn't mind the pain in his head, he could probably stand too. For now, though, he wanted to look at the light. It illuminated a wooden floor. He looked up. A man's height above his head, he saw the night sky through a square hole in the ceiling. The voices were coming from up there too.

Marco pulled his feet underneath him, then pushed himself up on shaking legs. The floor seemed to rock—to careen off behind him. He stumbled backward. His hands flailed behind him and found a dark, cool wall. Wooden. Marco rested there, wracked with dizziness. He wanted to yell, but the voices through the hole frightened him. In the darkness, Marco's brain knotted in confusion and fear. He didn't know where he was. The only human voices he could hear were voices he didn't understand. The square hole in the ceiling seemed the only way out of the room, but the hole terrified him. Furthermore, he was exhausted. And there, resting against the wall, Marco began to cry. The tears rose softly to his eyes, and slid down his dirty cheeks. His dry mouth coughed up quiet sobs.

Above him, Marco heard the voices go still. He froze, and covered his mouth with his hands. Silence. A voice began to speak. Other voices hushed it loudly. Silence. Then, the square of light in the ceiling went dark. So did the patch on the floor. He heard another voice, near enough that it made him jump. A man's face, he thought, covering the hole and looking down into the room—a man's voice, calling. Marco stayed quiet. The face disappeared, and Marco could see sky again. The moment of silence held for a second more.

Suddenly, all of the voices began talking at once. Marco's heart leaped to his throat. Like a great lid lifting, a much larger square opened in the ceiling. Moonlight spilled in—then brighter, yellow light—lantern light. Voices closed in around the yawning hole. Through it came a pair of legs, and then a waist, shoulders, and head. Man and lantern tumbled to the floor upon where Marco waited. The man stood and peered about. The lantern found

Marco almost at once. The man who held it was not much taller than Marco, but thicker. A muscular arm held the lantern in front of him. The man's feet and legs were bare. He had pulled his robe between his legs and tucked its hem into his wide belt. He wore a loose shirt over his arms and chest. His hair was thick, short, and dark. He looked at Marco, who stood trembling against the wall. Behind and above the man, a ring of faces looked in at the hatch. The man looked up at his companions. A grin creased his face. "*Granada!*" he said.

"*Granada!*" Shouted the faces above, and laughed. The man strode over to Marco, grabbed him by the wrist, and pulled him to the space of floor beneath the trap. In one move, he ducked below Marco's waist, and lifted the boy on his shoulder. Hands reached down from the trap. They grabbed Marco's arms and shirt. The man below him pushed Marco upward by the seat, and then by the calves, and then by the soles of his feet as rough hands pulled from above. As easily as a kitten lifted from a well, Marco found himself outside. The air around him was cool and salty.

"They've lifted me up through the roof," he thought. "What are they all doing up here on the roof?" Voices filled the night around him. They were laughing and calling to one another. Marco didn't understand a word. He looked up. Rising from the middle of the wooden floor where he lay was a tall post. The post rose up into the sky, as tall as six men together. Ropes hung down from the top of the pole—some were loose, some were taut, and some were tied to fixtures along the high rail that ran around the roof. Roof? Nerves knotted Marco's stomach. He heard the knock, knock of boots coming toward him on the wooden floor. He heard the padding of bare feet too. There were many men gathered around him now, talking and laughing one with another. Marco's brain screamed at him: *It's true, Marco! Get up and look.* Without thinking, Marco pushed himself to his feet. The man who had jumped down into the room with him hooked a foot around Marco's ankle and pushed him back to the floor. Marco had been on his feet for only a second. But in that second, he had seen what his brain had been shouting about. Gone were the drunken voices, loud and soft, of the *mercado* at night. Gone were the lamps in the *cabanas* that rose in a gentle slope, up and away from the wharf. Only stars remained, impossibly bright, in a vast cap that spread across the sky and down, down—ending in a seam along the low horizon— a seam between the starry cloth of the summer sky, and the black, buckling fabric of the ocean. Marco was at sea.

Chapter 2

The men standing above Marco moved about. Marco kept his face against the deck, and could see only their feet. Marco was on the monster ocean—the ocean that drank men down.

Marco groaned. "Father!" he cried out.

Above him he heard laughter. Someone groaned—like Marco had—and many laughed. The nausea that had risen in Marco since he woke up overcame him then. He retched on the deck, and the smell of vomit and salt made him retch again. One man made a distressed sound, as if he had broken an egg on a clean floor, or as if he had accidentally rolled a hot coal onto a good coat. A rough hand grabbed Marco by the wrist, and wrenched his arm above his head. The man whipped Marco quickly around, and dragged him across the deck toward the rail. Marco's feet slid through the vomit, and the men around him made a noise of amused disgust. Marco's man hoisted him roughly up. He pushed past the bony knees of slave rowers to the rail, where he held Marco out, all the way up to his stomach.

Marco's chest, arms, and head hung out over the black water. Marco screamed, but the scream choked in his throat as he vomited again. For many long moments, the man held Marco out over the rail. Head hanging down, Marco's brain whispered to him: *Yes, Marco, the sea. The sea. Black as you imagined, and more vast! The sea, Marco!* For long seconds, the man held him there. Then, when he was sure he would not be sick again, he nodded. The man pulled him back from the rail, and dropped him on the deck. Then he crossed to where Marco had been sick. Some laughed at the man.

The knot of men seemed to break up, some men going back to their beds, others back to their night duties, whatever they were. Marco watched his man as he crossed the deck. He was tall. Like the man who had dropped down into what Marco knew now as the ship's hold, the man's feet were bare. He wore a simple, straight robe that came down below his knees. His head was as bald as an egg. It shone in the moonlight. Marco watched the man take a bucket on a long rope. The man lowered it quickly over the side, and drew it heavily back up. He threw the water across the mess, and then lowered the bucket again. Some of the men were still laughing. Marco watched the water roll toward the gutter where the slaves rowed— opposite the gutter where he lay. As the water rolled, a pair of feet lifted to let it pass beneath them. Marco blinked. There was a man sitting on the rail across the deck. Marco had not noticed him before. Marco raised his eyes up the man's body. The man was in shadow, but Marco could see he was different than the other men. Marco could make out dark trousers, a light-colored shirt, and a long, open vest. Marco's eyes came to rest on the man's face. The man was looking at Marco. He had a short beard and hair pulled back from his head with a ribbon. The man's face was still as a stone. He did not move from the rail.

Suddenly, the bald man came between Marco and the bearded man. He took Marco by the wrist again, and dragged him forward, over the wet deck, toward the bow.

Other men were waiting for him there. One of the men was holding one end of a long rope, with a loop in one end. The rest of the rope lay in coils at the man's feet. The bald man held Marco's wrists together. The man with the rope slipped the loop around Marco's wrists. He drew the loop tight. Marco winced. Marco began to breathe more quickly, and his heart pounded. The men were talking all together now—talking and pointing up toward the foresail. All the while, the bald man held Marco by his bound wrists. After a moment some of the men nodded, as if they had reached an agreement. Someone took up the coils of the rope and disappeared behind the knot of men that had gathered around Marco. A moment later he returned, with just the end of the rope in his hands. He tugged the slack out of the rope. As he did, Marco's wrists jerked upward. Three other men stepped to the bare end of the rope, each grabbing onto it. Marco's eyes grew wide. With a yell, the four men on the rope pulled, hand over hand, over and over again in one steady motion. Marco's arms were yanked upward. The men on the rope whipped his body up off the deck like a doll. Marco screamed. The ship dropped beneath him, his stomach churning as he flew higher and higher. His arms burned. Marco gasped. Up the foresail he sped, until the knot that held his wrists thumped against the spar. Marco's arms absorbed the shock, and then the full weight of his body bounced beneath them. Marco's shoulders exploded in pain. Far below him, men pointed up and talked and argued. One man clapped his hands together and cheered as he looked up at Marco, hung in the rigging like a ham. Marco's vision began to blur. He was going to die now. He knew it. Tears of astonishment and fear sprang to his eyes. Marco watched them fall like little jewels down, down, down toward the distant deck. The men continued to point and argue. Marco began to sob. *The world is wide, and it is terrifying,* whispered his brain. *Why did you ever run from your friend in the mercado? Why did you ever look out toward the sea? What could your father have hoped to find here but horror?"* Marco interrupted his thoughts. "Pollito!" he sobbed. But Pollito was miles away, somewhere beyond the horizon. He could not joke with Marco here. He could not cajole Marco into finding a day's work, or make fun of him for staring out at the sea. Into Marco's thoughts of home swam a vision of his father's face. Hung in the rigging, Marco sobbed.

Then, without warning, the rope whirred over the spar, and Marco fell. The deck flew upward to meet him. Marco grit his teeth, bracing for impact. But in the moment before Marco smashed against the deck, the men who held the rope arrested his fall—they slowed his descent, so that when he fell to the deck, it only rattled his teeth instead of breaking his legs. Marco heard laughter and applause. "*Granada*," someone muttered. Others chuckled.

Off came the rope from his smarting wrists. The bald man grabbed his arm and dragged him back across the deck toward the hold. Only then, Marco noticed, did the bearded man on the rail move. He moved across the deck and reached out for Marco's other wrist. The bald man scolded him and pushed him back. The bearded man withdrew his hand from Marco's wrist, and reached down to open the hold door—the trap through which Marco had come. Again, the bald man pushed the bearded man away. Marco twisted his head around, only to see the bearded man disappear into the night shadows, shaking his head.

With one hand, the bald man pulled open the trap. With the other, he lifted Marco by the wrist, and lowered the boy through the hole. A foot-and-a-half above the floor, the man let go. Marco fell. His legs collapsed beneath him, and he lay still. Above him, the door slammed. Marco was surrounded by darkness again, darkness interrupted only by a small square of moonlight on the floor.

A long time had passed, Marco figured, when he became conscious again. Lying on the floor of the hold with his eyes closed, Marco didn't know if he was asleep or dead. His arms ached. His legs and torso were raw from where he had been dragged across the wooden deck. Pain washed about his lungs when he breathed. He lay there, and imagined the ocean as a great wall of black water that spread out around them. The ship, he thought, was like a tiny cork stuck in a hole. If the ship were to be plucked out, the ocean would burst through the hole it left—flooding the world. *So many terrifying ways to think about the sea,* though Marco.

"Are you awake?"

Marco was sure he had heard a voice. In the hold? Impossible.

"Boy. Are you awake?"

A voice. A voice that spoke Marco's Castilian.

"Un-uhnn," moaned Marco, too loudly.

"Be quiet if you want to talk," said the voice. "The watch is drunk and asleep, but there are plenty of others nearby. If they hear you, it's more of the same fun you remember."

"Fu-fun?" Marco slurred.

"Your trip up the foresail. That kind of fun."

Marco opened his eyes. The moonlight through the hold fell on the side of a bearded face.

"You ... above ... on deck ... "

"Yes, sitting on the gunwale. That's where you saw me. I tried to help you down gently, but *El Pelado* kept pushing me away."

"*El Pelado?*"

"*El Pelado*. The baldy. He's an oaf. But he's under orders to keep us apart. They don't want their new pet spoiled by their old parrot."

"Parrot?"

"I speak both the language of the Castilians and the language of the Moors. The kind *señores* on this tub bashed me on the head—much like they did to you, I imagine—and brought me aboard to deliver their vengeful warnings to anyone important they might snare."

"Do they ever snare anyone important?" Marco asked.

"Not yet," replied the bearded man. Marco hissed out what passed for a laugh.

"Funny?" scolded the stranger. "You might laugh so hard hung in the rigging. These men may not pose much of a threat to King Charles, but they can strip any fish like you or like me right down to the bone."

Discovering the identity of his visitor shook Marco fully awake. He tried to sit up. With effort, he rose up on his elbows, but could go no further.

"Lie still. You're nothing but aches, I shouldn't wonder," said the bearded man.

Marco let himself back down onto the floor. "They don't like people throwing up on their ship. I'll try to remember that," he said.

The bearded man gave a low chuckle. "You think that's why they flew you tonight?"

"I thought ... "

"They were practicing." The bearded man was silent for a moment. "It was a rehearsal, for the real thing tomorrow."

Marco stiffened. Real thing? Tomorrow? "What do you mean?" he croaked.

"What do you mean 'what do you mean'?" the bearded man was incredulous. "What kind of ship do you suppose this is?"

"*Piratas*," spat Marco.

"Well, maybe you're not an idiot then," said the man. "They're pirates, yes—and more than pirates. These pirates are Moors, on vengeance raids. Spanish slaves row this ship."

"Moors? What are Moors? Where did these pirates come from?" asked Marco.

"They came from our own home, boy," the bearded man answered.

"Our own home? What do you mean?"

"Time for a story, is it?" said the bearded man. "Very well—listen. You know Castile, Leòn ... all the provinces of Spain? You and I call them home. But forty generations ago, Moors—the ancient fathers of these pirates—came from the North of Africa and conquered our lands. For two centuries, the Moors ruled all that is now Spain. But Christian kings banded together, and with their armies drove the Moors—first out of one province, and then out of another. Over five centuries they did this. They finished their work the same year that Columbus sailed. Do you know anything about Columbus?"

"The Italian? I don't know much," said Marco.

"Only months before Columbus left our shores for the New World, our own Castilian knights fought against the Moorish fathers of these pirates, in a great battle at Granada. Juan Ponce de Leon fought as a knight in that battle, before he went across the sea. Do you know of Juan Ponce?"

Marco shook his head. "I have heard his name, but nothing more," he said.

The bearded man continued. "The battle of Granada gave the final piece back to us," he said, "and sent the last of the Moors into exile. That was almost thirty years ago. The fathers of these men went away, but not happy. Have you noticed that these pirates call you—"

"Granada," interrupted Marco.

"And I presume that's not your name."

"My name's Marco."

"Well, Marco, these men want to show your family and mine that just because we routed them doesn't mean that they won't fight back. Some few still sting us when they can. Granada isn't a nickname. It's a battle cry. They shout it to remember and to grow fierce."

"Are all Moors so?" said Marco, fearfully.

The bearded man shrugged. "Are all men like the men of one little band?" he said. "Even now, in the New World, Cortes and his Spanish armies lop off natives' heads with their big swords. Are all Spaniards so?" The man paused. "You know of Cortes?"

Marco shook his head. "I have heard his name, but nothing more."

The bearded man shrugged. "You know that Columbus was Italian, and you know nothing of Juan Ponce or Cortes. You have much to learn of the world, Marco. And while you are learning, learn this: hanging children by their wrists—sailing a ship rowed by Spanish slaves—may seem cruel. But prowling the coast of Africa are our ships—Spanish ships—with their galleys full of Moorish slaves, no doubt. Their kids swinging from our riggings too, I shouldn't wonder. Men are cruel everywhere, Marco."

There was silence between them for a moment. The man's words said themselves over and over in Marco's brain: *Men are cruel everywhere*. Thoughts about his father went through his head—thoughts about the million cruel things that may have befallen him. Then the bearded man spoke again. "Where did they collect you?"

"I live at Càdiz," said Marco.

"Tomorrow we near some port. This ship will likely be outnumbered twenty to one."

"Then tomorrow we are rescued?" asked Marco.

"Hardly," said the bearded stranger. "These men know that they only have one chance against a Castilian port— fear."

"I don't understand," said Marco.

"Maybe you are an idiot then. The crew of this ship means to hang you alive in a good, visible place in the rigging. They hope you'll scream. They hope to storm ships in sight of the port, with a screaming kid dangling from the yard. Were you a Castilian sailor, would you not be afraid to see such a thing—afraid enough to lose courage for a moment? Fear. That's your job tomorrow. And judging from tonight's performance, you'll likely do it well."

Marco could not speak.

"Tonight's fun was practice. The last kid lost a hand when they yanked him up. He fell to the deck, unconscious. He wasn't any use to them then. He died. They hope not to make the same mistake with you."

Marco still could not speak.

"Look," said the bearded man. "I don't owe you anything. I'm down here because the sot at watch is drunk and asleep, and I thought you should know what's in store. Countryman to countryman I come down here. Nothing more. If you have any courage, now is the time for it." He stood, and whispered, "If you had any guts, you'd chuck yourself overboard." Then Marco heard the man's soft boots on the ladder, and heard the big grate swing open and shut again.

"If you have any courage," the man had said. *But you haven't any*, said the voice in Marco's head. *You haven't any.*

Chapter 3

The light, shining through the hole in the ceiling, was bright on the floor of the hold where Marco lay. It was morning. Marco groaned. Almost as soon as he had made the noise, the great hatch opened. Sunlight filled the hold. Marco squinted, and raised a hand to shield his eyes. His shoulder hadn't ached until he tried to move it, but lifting his hand made Marco grimace in pain. There were voices above him. Someone grabbed at his raised hand and yanked him to his feet. Marco was lifted upward, into the cool morning. Strong hands dragged him across the deck and into the gutter where slaves waited to row. They left Marco in a pile against the gunwale, next to the rowers. The crew was busy. Marco looked through bleary eyes as men hurried about the deck. They tied knots and checked swords and shoved cannons into place. Marco tried to clear his vision by blinking. Before him, an arm's length away, was the coiled rope. Marco shuddered. He lifted his eyes and looked out over the deck. Two sets of wooden stairs led from the main deck up to the quarterdeck. Beneath one of them, in shadow, Marco saw the bearded man. Their eyes met, but the bearded man didn't blink or raise an eyebrow. Marco began to wonder if their meeting last night in the hold had been nothing but a dream.

Marco was startled from his thoughts by a shout from the crow's nest. He twisted his neck painfully upward. The man on watch was shouting down toward the deck. His finger wagged at a point off the starboard bow. Men on deck sprang into desperate action. The pitch of the shouting rose, and Marco imagined himself hoisted up ahead of the foresail. It would happen any moment. *El Pelado* would come and take him by the hands and tie them with the rope.

The rowers around him had begun to move. Pulling against their great oars, they were turning the ship toward the place where the man in the crow's nest pointed. Knees and elbows flailed around Marco. He looked again at the bearded man beneath the stairs. The man's face remained a stone, even amid the confusion of the crew. As he looked at the man, the noise around Marco seemed to stop. For a moment, all Marco could hear were the words the man had spoken last night: "*If you had any guts, you'd chuck yourself overboard.*" The words seemed to twist Marco's courage in a knot. The voice in his head screamed—*overboard? Into the sea? The vast, terrible sea? Estàs loco, hermanito!* Marco's imagination exploded with a vision of his father, drowning in the terrible sea. Marco's heart leaped to his throat. His limbs shook. The movement on deck was furious now— men running and shouting and flinging ropes and grabbing swords. Marco glanced again at the man under the stairs. He was staring at Marco. Under the man's stare, Marco willed his muscles to stillness. Then, slamming every door of thought in his screaming mind, he lunged between the rowers' limbs. "*Oh Dios! Socorro!* God help me!" he screamed. He pushed up with all his might on his sore legs. He launched himself upward and backward. The gunwale caught him in the back of the knees, and he kicked a rower in the arm as he tumbled backward, but in an instant he was over the side. Plummeting toward the water, he caught the long shaft of an upward-bound oar in the ribs. The oar did not break, but jerked downward, flinging Marco clumsily into the water. Above him on the ship, he thought, a rower surely got the short end of the oar in the teeth.

Beneath the water, Marco flailed. He could not swim, and didn't know whether his thrashing was driving him toward the surface or driving him deeper down into the black ocean.

His lungs were empty. His heart pounded between them. He opened his mouth in a silent scream. Only bubbles came out. The water around him was filled with them. Then, from under the water, Marco heard a great splash. Nearby, something—or someone—had fallen from the ship. In an instant, a strong arm went around his neck and wrenched him upward. When Marco's head broke the surface, the world changed. The roar of the deep ocean was replaced with the sounds of shouting and of oars slapping the water. Marco could not see the man who held him. But he heard the man shouting. It was the bearded stranger. He had leaped into the water after Marco, and was shouting at the ship. They were behind the ship, off the stern to starboard. The bearded man's arm was tightly around Marco's neck. It was better than being underwater, but

Marco was having difficulty breathing. Marco could not understand the words that the bearded man was saying, but the man shouted them over and over.

Marco couldn't move his head in the grip of the bearded man, and his breath whistled through a windpipe that felt as if it would be crushed any second. *Does he know he's crushing my throat?* thought Marco. *Am I to die in the very act of being rescued?*

Marco grabbed onto the man's arm. He struggled to break the man's grip. Something hard pressed into the back of his head. Bone-hard. Rock hard. Whatever it was, it bruised him terribly. But his rescuer was busy shouting at the ship. *He must not notice what he's doing!* thought Marco. He couldn't speak.

The boy rolled his eyes, hoping to see what was around them. He first saw the ship, and it looked like it was getting further away. He could still hear shouts, and see some of the men running on the ship's deck. Other men looked over the rail, pointing at Marco and the man who held him. A sudden sound made the hair on Marco's neck prickle. CRACK! The noise was huge—louder than a thunderclap. The men on the deck turned their attention instantly away from Marco, and were now looking at something else, off the ship's starboard bow. Marco rolled his eyes that way. Churning up the ocean in the distance was another ship, a great wooden hull rising from the waves. It was close enough that Marco could hear the shouts of the men on its deck. He understood the words.

"*Esperan ... esperan! Wait! Listos? Ready? Fuego!*" Another CRACK, as a cannon fired. Marco heard the whistling of a cannonball and the sound of splintering wood. The pirate ship had been hit.

The cannon fire stopped the bearded man from shouting at the slave ship. Now he was shouting at the other ship. "*Socorro! Miren aqui! Help! Look here!*" His grip on Marco's throat had not lessened, and Marco was beginning to feel dizzy. The blue sky began to go dark above him. He could no longer feel the cold of the water around him. The voice of the bearded man, together with the sounds of the battling ships, began to fade.

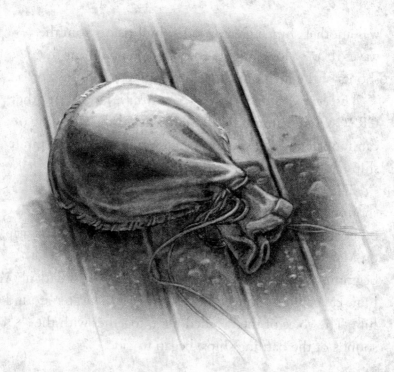

Chapter 4

Marco heard the sound of gulls. He was awake, but his eyes were still closed. He lay on his back and listened. Above him somewhere, someone laughed. He could hear talking, too. It sounded like it was miles away.

Marco's head rested on something soft. He was warm and dry. He rested for what felt like a long time with his eyes closed. No one tried to grab him by the arms or tie him up. He tried to remain quiet. He was so tired. So very tired ...

———

Marco dreamed. In his dream, he saw his father's face. It was drowning. Hair swirled around the face. His father's eyes were wide and staring in terror and rage, and his mouth was open in a silent scream. His father's clothes were dark and wet. They billowed in the freezing water. Marco's father reached out a hand, his fingers stretched in panic and fear. Then, in Marco's dream, hands reached out to Marco's father. Everything went white.

Marco opened his eyes. The dream was gone, and he was awake. He could not see the water. He could not see his father. He saw blue sky, crisscrossed by the dark lines of a ship's rigging. He saw enormous white sails, folded under thick spars. He felt warm sun on his face. A cool wind came in little gusts across his face and through his hair. Marco blinked. He heard a voice.

"See there? It's not as you thought, Garrido."

A second voice, "He's not well yet, Alonso. I still say he's as good as dead."

"Nonsense," said the first voice. "Before long, he'll be awake and alive, and I'll be collecting on our wager." There were sounds of good-natured laughter at this. Marco could not keep his eyes open. They drifted shut. He heard "Oh you see, there he goes again. Maybe tomorrow ... " but he didn't know which voice had said it, and he didn't hear any more.

—

Marco twitched, and the twitch woke him up. If he had dreamed, he could not remember. Around him, no one stirred. He opened his eyes. It was very dark, but he could see that he was in a bunk. A wool blanket was tucked snugly around him. Soft, yellow lantern light lit the shelf in the wall where his bunk lay. There was a pillow beneath his head. Out beyond the bunk, somewhere off across the ship's forecastle, he could hear soft voices. He blinked his eyes to focus them. Nearby, Marco saw stacks of casks, and square wooden boxes. Shadows moved along the boxes and casks—shadows cast by a dim lantern off in the direction of the voices. Marco lay still. He could hear them talking.

"You saw how he held the boy," said one voice, "it was not the grip of a rescuer. It was a cruel grip."

"Come now," said another voice. "The sea was about to draw them both down. Ships battled above them. One cannot think of being gentle when flailing in the sea."

"You heard what he said, though?" asked the first voice.

"Yes, I heard. Delirium. The confused babble of a dire

moment," said the second voice. "They were both drowning."

Marco knew that the men were arguing about the bearded rescuer—and that Marco himself was the boy in their conversation. He wondered where the bearded man was now.

"But think—a free Castilian aboard a Moorish slave ship? Explain it! You cannot, can you? Nor can I," said the first voice.

"He had been captured and forced to interpret for the raiders," said the second voice. "Listen, Garrido. You see shadows around corners where there are no shadows. You sweat, watching for enemy ships in every fog. The boy was saved, and the boy was saved. This is all. And the man risked his life to do it."

"But Alonso, listen to reason, I beg of you!"

"Quiet, Garrido! I have had enough," said Alonso. "To speak of conspiracy against the boy is to look for the devil in the face of a baby. He's a waif—a wharf rat. He has nothing. There is no cruel man that would pay a moment's attention to the boy—to speak nothing of leaping into the ocean after him."

"I know he's a wharf rat, Alonso!" hissed Garrido. "But I do not believe that the stranger meant to save the boy."

"But he did save me," said Marco suddenly. His voice

rattled up through his throat like dust in a dry barrel. It was barely above a whisper, and it hurt his throat when he said it. It was as if he had not spoken through his throat for weeks. *How long have I been asleep?* he wondered.

The middle deck went silent.

"Did you hear that?" it was Alonso who spoke.

"The boy!" whispered Garrido. There was the sound of scrambling feet and of barrels and casks being shoved aside. In a moment, a lantern was shoved in front of Marco's face. Marco shut his eyes against the sudden light. Again, he heard voices.

"See, he sleeps still," said the voice of Garrido.

"Idiot," said Alonso, "His eyes are closed because you've got the lantern in his face. Move it." There was silence for a moment. During the silence, Marco waited. Were these friends or enemies? One spoke ill of Marco's rescuer, and they had both called Marco a wharf rat. On the slave ship, the bearded man had spoken of Castilian ships rowed by Moorish slaves. Could this be such a ship? What were the chances of getting caught in the crossfire between two outlaw slave ships and escaping one only to be brought aboard another? His thoughts turned to his mother—dead under a high fever. They turned to his father—lost at sea. *Why should my luck change now?* he thought.

Why indeed. The lantern-light played still on his closed

eyelids, and he feared to open them. He waited a long time. The lantern remained. Or did it? Maybe he was imagining the warm light on his face. Maybe the men had moved away again. Marco itched. Why had he said anything at all? *Stupid, stupid Marco*, he thought. He wondered if he could open his eyes just a tiny crack—enough to see if the men were still there, but not enough for them to notice. Risky. Slowly, Marco parted his eyelashes just enough to let light in.

"There, you see! He is awake!" said Alonso.

"Hello, boy," said Garrido. Marco gave up. He opened his eyes. The faces of the two men were only inches away from his own.

The face on the left—the face that belonged to the voice of Alonso—was clean-shaven. It was a large, long face, with a wide mouth and a tangle of grey hair above it. Its skin was like soft leather. Lines had worn themselves into it. It was an old face, but strong looking—ruddy and sun-swept.

The other face—the face that belonged to the voice of Garrido, was as bald on top as *El Pelado* had been, with sprouts of black hair above his ears. The face was soft and dark. His ears poked out on the sides of his head. His eyebrows arched like little rainbows above his round eyes. Both men were smiling.

———

La Juana was a big, sturdy ship. It was bound for San Juan Bautista, the big island in the West. Some called it *Puerto Rico*—the rich port. Alonso spent his time counting and cataloguing what was in the hold. Garrido spent his time puffing back and forth, tending to the great sails. He climbed up and down the shrouds—the great cords that held the mast. He marked speed.

Still, even with all the work, Alonso and Garrido found time to visit Marco in the dimly lit forecastle where his bunk lay. They made him laugh, mostly. Alonso knew funny and exciting stories about farmers and sailors and wars. He sang Marco a song about fifteen camels that had been caught in a spider web. In the song, the camels kept calling to more camels for help, and the camels that came to help all wound up stuck in the spider web, too.

Garrido knew many funny tricks, and did them to make Marco laugh. He borrowed empty bottles from the galley, and then would suck the bottles onto his lips so they'd stick. Sometimes he could stick a bottle to his lips, and then slide it onto his cheek and dangle it there. It was a strange trick. He borrowed eggs from the ship's chickens, and could make it appear as if they were coming out of his mouth one by one. Once, an egg broke all over Garrido's chin. Marco fell out of his bunk, laughing.

Marco loved visits from Alonso and Garrido. His fear of the sea faded some, perhaps because he had not seen it since his rescue. His adventure among the Moorish pirates had weakened him, and in the first days of his time aboard *La Juana*, he never left his bunk. It was easy to be brave in his bunk. What would happen when he was well enough to walk the deck?

When Alonso and Garrido were away, Marco found himself thinking about the man who had rescued him. That man had not visited him. As far as Marco knew, he had not seen his rescuer since the day of the rescue. The man may have been among those who came to sleep and talk in the forecastle. If so, he had never stopped to talk to Marco.

But Marco imagined him.

Marco's imagination about the man was fueled by the conversation he had heard between Alonso and Garrido. He had heard words like "cruel." Could the man have been plotting against Marco somehow? And why? It hurt Marco's head to think about. Thoughts of the mysterious man often exhausted Marco, and he would fall asleep—into fitful dreams.

Early one morning, Alonso came to Marco's bunk. He whipped the wool blanket from the boy, and left Marco stretching and scratching his head.

"Today, boy, you come up into the sun. I will introduce you to the captain. It is by his gracious pleasure that you are a guest aboard *La Loca.*"

"Isn't the ship called *"La Juana"*? Marco asked as he pulled on his shirt.

Alonso only laughed.

Holding Alonso's hand, Marco took his first steps since the rescue. Together, they walked to the door that led from the forecastle. On deck, Marco squinted his eyes against the sun. Alonso cleared his throat, and some of the men on deck turned and clapped or hollered. Marco blushed.

"You are a celebrity," said Alonso to Marco. "The boy that we snatched from the pirates."

"Then we won?" asked Marco.

"Hardly a victory," said Alonso, "Except for you. The other ship—we surprised her. We are a big ship, but we have few cannons. This is a supply ship, not a war ship."

"What happened to the pirates, then?"

Alonso shrugged. "We shouted and fired at them until we pulled you from the water, and then we sailed by. The encounter was brief, and they did not pursue us." Alonso looked up. Two men crossed the deck in front of Alonso. One wore tall boots and a long coat. Walking with him was a man in dark trousers, a linen shirt, and a long, open vest.

He also had a beard—a beard that Marco recognized. "Ah, here comes the captain," said Alonso. "Captain Herrera!"

The man in the long boots turned. His hair was close-cropped. His face was clean-shaven. His coat covered broad shoulders and a chest like a barrel. The bearded man stopped with him.

"Yes?" said the captain—the clean-shaven man.

Alonso pointed to Marco.

"Ah," said Captain Herrera. "The boy seems to be on his feet." He spoke to the bearded man. "A happy ending to that part of your story then, Señor Matanza."

"Indeed," said the bearded man. He nodded to Marco, "Hello, boy."

"Hello, Señor ... Matanza?"

"Matanza, yes."

"Thank you for rescuing me, Señor Matanza."

Señor Matanza shrugged. "We both came out ahead, it would seem," he said.

The captain spoke, "You will continue to keep him out of trouble, Alonso?"

"Surely," said Alonso. "The boy is no trouble at all. Good as gold. Disastrous on the shrouds, I'll wager, and I'd not put him in the crow's nest until he's got his legs—but I can find something for him, I'm sure."

Marco didn't know what Alonso meant.

"Good, then," said the captain. He turned to Matanza. "Continue please. You say the best price comes from ... " their talk was lost to Marco as he watched them walk away.

Alonso turned to Marco. "Enough for today, yes?"

Marco nodded. He was glad of the sunshine and the sea air, but his head was light and his knees unsteady. Alonso gently shepherded Marco back to his bunk, and sat beside him.

"So this Matanza. He is the man who rescued me?" said Marco

Alonso answered, mimicking Matanza's voice.

"Indeed," he said.

"Yes," grinned Marco, "Exactly." And then, more seriously, "When first I woke up on my first day aboard *La Juana*, I heard you and Garrido talking about him."

"Yes."

"What sort of man is he?" asked Marco.

"A difficult man to figure out." answered Alonso.

Marco stared, hoping for more information.

Alonso relented. "When we first saw you in the water, he shouted something over and over, as he held you around the throat. But he was not shouting at us. He was shouting at the pirates, in their language. I don't understand much of the language of the Moors, but he seemed to be shouting, 'I have him! I have him!'"

"I don't know what you mean," said Marco, confused.

"At first, we believed—and by 'we' I mean myself and my fat friend Garrido—that he had some plot against you. That perhaps you were some important boy and he was hoping to profit in some way by keeping you in the hands of the pirates—that he was in league with them."

"And now?"

Alonso shrugged. "We still believe the same thing. Except for the part about Matanza being in league with the pirates." Alonso looked at Marco. "And the part about you being an important boy." He poked Marco in the ribs with a grin. Marco smiled too.

"Stop tickling. I am trying to understand," said Marco.

"Matanza isn't in league with the pirates. We have had him aboard for a week now—"

"It's been a week?" interrupted Marco.

"A week. And in the week, we learned that Matanza is in league with no one but Matanza. He thinks of no one's skin but his own. To bring you back to the pirates would have put him in their favor. You were important only for that. He did not suspect that we would rescue you both, and escape the pirates altogether."

"Important only for that ... " muttered Marco.

"I have offended you?" asked Alonso. "Take no offense! Here aboard *La Juana* none of us is anyone. Rats on a supply ship, no more. But you? You are our victory prize! A reason to cheer and to drink more than usual."

Marco laughed at this.

"As for Matanza," continued Alonso, "see how he follows Captain Herrera about? He flatters him from hour to hour, and even now tries to convince him to stop carting stores between Spain and the New World and to fill his hold with Indian slaves instead. Like Juan Ponce de Leon does in San Juan, he says. More profit for an able captain, he says."

Marco shuddered. He had been close enough to slavery to last the rest of his life, he thought.

"Have you seen his pouch?" asked Alonso.

"His pouch?" Marco blinked. His short trip above-decks had wearied him, but he wanted to hear more.

"He has a pouch of gold coins beneath his shirt. He filched them one by one from those pirates while he was aboard," chuckled Alonso. "Brandishes the pouch when he wants to look important. Holds the coins up to the light. Likes to lord it over us that way."

"I think I got that pouch in the back of the head when he rescued me," said Marco. The bruise from the rescue remained sore and swollen.

"Silly," said Alonso.

"Silly?" The word was difficult to say. Marco was

slipping into sleep.

"Silly," said Alonso. "On a ship, a whole basket of coins won't get any of us anything more than what we've got coming. Won't make the wind blow faster, and won't improve the taste of the dinner stew. We're all ignoring that purse, and I think it's stuck in his craw. He wants us to notice and to be impressed. Sullen, he is."

"Sullen ... purse ... Matanza ... " said Marco, and then closed his eyes.

———

The days aboard *La Juana* were warm, and Marco slipped in and out of them as if they were a dream. The sailors were friendly, and when he felt strong he would go above-deck and talk with them. Day by day he grew stronger, and soon he was able to help with simple tasks on the ship.

"You call the ship *La Loca*—'the crazy woman'," he said one day to Garrido. "Alonso does it too. But the ship is called *La Juana*. I do not understand the joke."

Garrido chuckled. "We call her *La Loca* for the queen. You know—*La Reina Juana*."

Marco looked puzzled.

"You know," said Garrido, "Isabela's idiot daughter. Queen of Castile, you know?"

Marco didn't know. On land, he had slept on the street or on the floor in Pollito's cottage. He worried for his next meal—or for his father. He did not know who wore the crowns in the stone *castillos*. He had always scoffed at knowing such things—what did it help him at dinnertime to know how kings and queens fared in their palaces? But now, at sea, the whole world of things that Marco did not know spread out like the ocean around him. It frightened him. Still, he chuckled thinly.

"Oh, yes. *That* Juana. *La Loca*. Of course."

On another day, he helped Alonso to scrub the salt from the gunwale.

"How long before we reach San Juan?" Marco asked.

"You grow weary of our trip aboard *La Juana*?" Alonso smiled.

"No," said Marco, "I like it aboard ship."

"This is because you are the pet of the crew and you have no chores," said Alonso. "For most of us, being at sea is hard work." He grunted as he scrubbed.

"I can see that," said Marco. "I'm not blind. You want me to work harder?"

Alonso stopped scrubbing, "No, little one. If you worked harder, you might stop talking. I like talking to you."

"I like talking to you, too," said Marco.

They both fell silent. They scrubbed. They scrubbed some more.

"You like talking to me," said Alonso, "so you stop talking?"

"I am wondering now," said Marco.

"What are you wondering?" asked Alonso.

"A week ago," said Marco, "I was at home in Càdiz."

"It was more like a month ago," said Alonso. "But go on."

A month ago? Marco's eyes went wide. Had he lost track of time so completely?

"Well, go on," said Alonso.

"A month ago, then," muttered Marco, "After that, I was a slave. And now I am a sailor."

"Yes," Alonso chuckled. "A mighty sailor. Scrub the patch around that bit, will you?"

Marco continued. "When we get to San Juan, what will I be then? This is what I am wondering."

"Who knows," said Alonso. "Great spiders from Castilian ports sometimes crawl into the boxes that go to the colonies, and then live long lives on bananas in San Juan. Perhaps you will crawl off of this ship and into a life of great ease. It is the New World, after all."

Marco smiled and shook his head. "Addled," he said. "The ship gets its nickname from you, crazy old man—not from the queen."

"You think I am not serious?" said Alonso. "I have seen strange things. What if we pull into port, and Juan Ponce himself is there to greet us. He sees a skinny boy and says, 'this is just the boy to feed my horses. You, boy, come over here! Would you like a job?' Then, because you are an obedient boy and because he is a great man, you go. And you live the rest of your life eating good food and sleeping in a warm bed in Juan Ponce's big white house." It was a funny story—Alonso had told it to make Marco laugh. But Marco had fallen serious.

"Juan Ponce?"

"Juan Ponce, the most important man in San Juan. You don't know who he is?"

"Him I know," said Marco. "Fought in the battle of Granada. Sailed with Columbus."

"This is all you know of him?"

Marco nodded.

"Pity," said Alonso. "It would have been a funnier story if you had known."

"Tell me," said Marco.

"It is too long," muttered Alonso.

"We have much salt to scrub away," said Marco, "and if I am to feed his horses for the rest of my life, I must know, mustn't I." He grinned.

"Juan Ponce is a slaver." The voice came from behind them. Marco spun around to find Matanza, munching on a piece of dried fish.

"A slaver? Nonsense," said Alonso. "Explorer. Governor. Not slaver."

"Nonsense?" retorted Matanza. "How many balls, fired from Juan Ponce's guns, have come to rest in the brains of natives in the New World? How many Taino have died under the hooves of his horses? How many Caribs? How many have been forced to work the mines to fill Juan Ponce's coffers?"

"You ask me four questions before I can answer even one," growled Alonso. "But—"

"Caribs?" questioned Marco. "Taino?"

Matanza answered him. "The Taino are the native people of the Islands that Juan Ponce now rules with a bloody fist. The Caribs come from the South and the East. The Caribs would do to Juan Ponce what Juan Ponce has done to the Taino—but he crushes them, too. He crushes them all."

"You are too hasty," interrupted Alonso, "to describe Juan Ponce de Leon as a thug."

"You think I do it out of disrespect?" snapped Matanza. "On the contrary, I have nothing but deep admiration for Juan Ponce. These are the things that will bring us glory in

the New World—conquer the weak, sell some of the
survivors as slaves, and use the rest to work the mines and
the farms. The bounty of their labors is destined to be ours.
Juan Ponce knows this," said Matanza. "As for me, I go to
him as soon as I can. *La Juana* is the passage to glory that I
never knew I had. This purse," he tapped his chest and
Marco could hear the clink of coins, "is bound to grow
when we reach San Juan—if there are any Taino left to sell."

"Boy," said Alonso, turning to Marco, "Matanza doesn't
know what he's talking about. Don't imagine Juan Ponce as
a tyrant—"

"And don't you imagine him as a priest!" said Matanza.
"Those who pretend that the New World will be won with
kindness will be crushed beneath the wheels of self-interest
and might. Those will make the difference in this new
land."

Matanza threw a fishbone over the ship's side, and then
moved away. Alonso watched him, but did not speak.

"Self-interest? Might? What does he mean?" said Marco.

"He means that if you are a strong man and look out
for no one but yourself you can make a lot of money by
selling everyone else short. That's all he means. Matanza is
for Matanza."

"It sounded more convincing when Matanza said it,"
muttered Marco.

"Then maybe you are still sick," said Alonso. "Do not listen to idiots when you are sick."

Alonso whacked his cleaning brush on the gunwale, and walked away. Marco sat for a moment, then walked back toward the forecastle. The conversation had exhausted him. The sun had begun to set, and great clouds were rolling toward them. Far away on the sea, it was raining.

When he descended the stairs, he saw someone sitting next to his bed. It was Garrido.

"Ah, I've been waiting for you," said the sailor. Marco was happy to see him. Garrido had a stick in his hand, and a tin plate. "Watch this, boy." He held the stick up in the air, and balanced the plate on the end of the stick. Marco applauded. Garrido stopped him by holding up a finger. Then Garrido took the plate in his hand, and tossed it, spinning, into the air. He caught the plate, still spinning, on the end of the stick. Marco hooted. Garrido grinned. "You were above decks longer than usual today," he said. "You are getting stronger."

"I was talking with Alonso and Matanza," said Marco.

"Alonso and Matanza do not talk," said Garrido. "It would be interesting to have heard this conversation."

"Not so interesting," said Marco. "They argued about Juan Ponce."

"Juan Ponce, the treasure-hunter?"

"No, Juan Ponce de Leon, of San Juan," answered Marco.

"Sì *Señor*, the treasure hunter!" grinned Garrido.

"The slaver, says Matanza. The kindly explorer, says Alonso."

Garrido frowned. "Slaver?" He shrugged. "Explorer?" He shrugged again. "All I know about him is that he found a mountain of gold. The natives pull it from the hill for him in San Juan. With all his gold, he can ask what he wants. It is for him that we go to San Juan. *La Loca* carries spices and cloth for the colony, and swords for Juan Ponce."

"Swords?" asked Marco

Garrido shrugged. "A few swords, yes. We have seeds with us too. And plants grown up from seeds. And shovels. And saws, and axes." Garrido fell silent. Marco watched him.

Garrido spoke again. "The whole sea is on fire with news of the New World. Good men are going. Bad men are going. Crazy men are going. Some women are going, too."

"Crazy men?" asked Marco.

"Look at you. Look at me," joked Garrido. Marco laughed. Garrido was silent again. Then he spoke.

"Señor Columbus discovered something—little islands. That is what he brought to us. But Juan Ponce has found something bigger—a giant island, bigger than Spain.

Beautiful beyond words. Lovely like flowers at Easter. For this he calls the place *La Florida*. The crown has given him permission to go on another great treasure-hunting trip. Perhaps I will go too. And if I cannot go with Juan Ponce, I will go further, and join Cortes."

"Cortes? Who is Cortes?" asked Marco.

Garrido laughed. "You are a little frog still in an egg if you do not know who Cortes is." Garrido sighed. "Cortes is a mighty man. He is stronger than Juan Ponce."

"How do you know? Have you met him?"

"Juan Ponce sits in peace in San Juan tending to his farms and to his daughters, while Cortes slashes his way with swords through the middle of the great island."

"Cortes sounds frightening," said Marco.

"More frightening than Juan Ponce," said Garrido. "He does more."

"You mean to say that Juan Ponce is lazy?"

Garrido paused. "No, little one. Even now, Juan Ponce is restless. He wishes to sail again himself."

"So Juan Ponce wants—"

"Gold! He wants gold of course, child. What else is there?"

Treasure hunter? Slave-driving bully? Benevolent governor? Marco's friends' words were all he knew of Juan Ponce de Leon, and Juan Ponce was all he knew of San

Juan—and San Juan, this place of slaves and spiders, bananas and gold, was to be his next home. Marco tried to imagine Juan Ponce in his mind, but he kept seeing his father instead. Marco missed him more than ever.

A cry broke loudly into Marco's thoughts: "All hands! All hands!" The floor beneath Marco tipped. Garrido tumbled backward off of his stool. The tin plate went clattering across the forecastle. The man clambered to his feet and chugged toward the stairs. "Stay here, boy!" he shouted over his shoulder.

But Marco couldn't. Wide-awake now, he slipped from his bed, across the forecastle, and out the door. The sky was dark now, the twilight further muffled by the black clouds descending on the ship. A sudden and fierce headwind had caught the mainsail and the foresails, and as Marco struggled for balance, the ship yawed wildly. Stinging rain fell, roaring on the deck.

Across the deck, lashing gear to the soaked ship, was Alonso. The old man saw him. "Go below, Marco!" he shouted.

"What?" Marco yelled through the storm. At that moment, the sail went slack. The bowsprit jerked forward and downward, dropping the bow of the ship toward the rolling ocean, in the trough of a great wave. The ship plunged downward, and a wall of water exploded over the deck. Swept from his feet, Marco screamed. Tumbled along with gear and men, he slammed against the inside of the gunwale. Water gargled in his mouth, and plastered his hair across his forehead and into his eyes. Marco hoisted himself to his feet and wiped the water from his face with a trembling hand.

He staggered along the gunwale, back toward the forecastle door. The rain came in sheets, and it was hard to see. All around him, men shouted as they hauled on ropes. Above him, a man lost his grip on a wet line, and was tossed from his perch as the ship dove over the crest of a wave. He fell to the deck and hollered in pain. Ahead of him, Marco thought he could see Matanza. The bearded man was on one knee, wrapping a rope back and forth around a cleat. Marco froze and held to the gunwale. Matanza's hand slipped again and again on the rope, and he muttered words that Marco could not hear over the sound of the water around him. Above Matanza's head, Marco watched a rope whip loose in the gale. It left a spar to flail in the wind. From elsewhere on deck, Garrido had seen it too. He staggered to the rope, and reached for the swinging spar. His hand snatched at it, but it swung out of reach. Just then, Matanza finished with the rope, and pushed himself to his feet.

"*Cuidese Señor!* Look out!" Garrido shouted the words at

the top of his lungs, but they were no more than a whisper above the storm. The spar caught Matanza in the back of the neck. He pitched forward and hit the deck on his hands and knees. For a moment, he was still. Then, as Marco watched, Matanza shook his head, steadied himself on the gunwale, and stood again. Behind him, Garrido's plump hands had found the rope and lashed the spar safely aside. Rain running in rivulets down his face, Garrido glanced at Marco through the storm and winked. Marco began to move again, his hands clutching at the gunwale. Ahead of him moved Matanza, heading aft.

Suddenly, with a great squeal of twisting wood, the prow of the ship arched up over a monstrous black hill of water. Garrido toppled backward, his arms spinning like windmills. Marco's legs slipped out from beneath him, but he gripped the gunwale with all his strength. Ahead of him, Matanza reached wildly for something to steady him, and found Garrido's spar. Water running down his face and off his beard, Matanza gripped it. It pulled against the line that held it. The line yanked itself taut, shuddering under the weight of the bearded man. Then Marco heard the snap. The line whipped up and away in the wind. The spar, propelled by Matanza's full weight, swung violently back toward him. It struck him on the neck and collarbone, spinning him a quarter-turn toward the prow. Matanza fell to one knee, clutching at his Adam's apple. Marco watched as the man scrambled for the gunwale—watched as he flung his arms around it. His back was now to Marco. Marco lowered his eyes to the deck.

In a tiny sopping heap on the deck, between the man and the boy, lay Matanza's pouch. Marco's eyes widened. Its cord must have been cut when the spar struck the man. The pouch must have slid through the man's shirt when he fell to the deck. Matanza had not yet noticed its absence. As the ship righted itself, Marco let go of the gunwale and pounced on the little bag. He looked up at Matanza. The man still had not turned. He reached out to tap the man on the shoulder—to hand him the soaked pouch. But then his hand—outstretched toward Matanza's back—stopped. Thoughts in Marco's brain ran wild. Marco remembered the market—Pollito's hands, balanced in the air to teach him a lesson: one hand for work, and one hand for the money that came from it. He wondered what work had brought the contents of the pouch to Matanza. Surely nothing so balanced as selling milk for a profit. At sea, things were different. He had watched men throw their backs honorably into hoisting sails or scrubbing the salt from the deck—dutifully filling the measure of their employ—only to watch them pilfer rum from the ship's stores in the dead of night. At sea, when it was time for the crew to work as one man, they did it. Lines were run, prows were turned—the ship was like a machine, and the sailors its working parts. But beyond the work of sailing the ship, they were not one man at all. They were many, and each had designs on his own fortune. Such was the economy of the sea. A boy might have turned over a lost pouch to his betters. But there, with the storm whipping the water into Marco's eyes—there, facing the heaving back of the injured Matanza, Marco decided it was time for something different. It was time for Marco to stop being a boy, and to care for his own fortune.

Marco clutched the pouch to his breast and tottered through the pounding rain away from the gunwale, toward the door to the forecastle. He was thinking about Pollito. Someday, he would show him the pouch. Someday he would see the surprised look on Pollito's face when he saw Marco's fortune. Pollito's parents would laugh and clap him on the back. It would be Marco's turn to balance his hands in the air—one hand for adventure, and one for the opportunity that came with it. Marco grinned, lost for a moment in thought. Behind him, he did not see the moment of realization in Matanza's face. He did not see Matanza grope inside his shirt or look frantically about the deck, before narrowing his eyes on the boy disappearing into the darkness of the forecastle.

Marco's heart pounded as he stumbled back through the creaking crates to his little bunk. He shoved Matanza's pouch deep beneath the loose straw mattress that covered the planks of his bed. Above him, he could hear muffled shouts as men battled the storm. He could still lend a hand there, he thought. He took a deep breath, and turned.

Matanza's face was six inches from his own. The man swung his arms out and grabbed Marco's shoulders. Marco howled.

"Where is it, son?" Matanza growled. He closed his eyes tightly and shook his head as if trying to shake off a sharp headache.

Marco screamed again, "*Socorro!* Help!"

"Shut up!" hissed Matanza. "Give me back what you took."

"I don't know what you're talking about!" spat Marco. He squirmed in Matanza's grip.

"Do you think I am an idiot?" Matanza was shouting now. One powerful hand went to Marco's neck. As Matanza's anger swelled, he pushed Marco by the throat toward the wall. "Who do you think you're talking to, boy?"

"*Socorro!*" choked Marco. He could barely hear the words himself. His head was against the wall now, and Matanza's hand pressed harder and harder, crushing the air from the boy's lungs. The edges of Marco's vision began to blur, and then to go black. "Help ... " he whimpered again. This time, no sound came out at all.

Just as Marco's consciousness began to slip, Matanza's grip was broken. The man stumbled backward. Marco coughed and sputtered. He put his hands to his aching windpipe. As his vision cleared, he saw an arm around Matanza's chest. Another hand swiped from behind, pulling Matanza's arms backward.

"Come now, *Señor!*" Marco recognized the voice. It was Alonso. Matanza spun free of the powerful arms. He turned to face his attacker.

"Keep your 'Come now,' dog!" snarled Matanza. "The boy has stolen from me. I'll have it back now."

"See reason, friend," said Alonso. "The ship leans in a storm that cares nothing for what is yours or what is mine. Spend your strength on deck battling the storm."

"I'll come when I have what the boy took!" barked Matanza.

"We speak of this later, yes? Should the ship sink in this gale, will you be the idiot shouting at a ten-year-old as fishes swim by?"

Alonso looked at Matanza. Matanza looked at Alonso.

Behind both of them came a clattering of crates and a shout.

"Alonso! *Señores!* Please, will you come now?" Garrido

had come into the forecastle.

Matanza was outnumbered. Teeth clenched, he turned toward Marco. "We are not yet finished with this," he said, and he put a finger in Marco's chest. Then he turned and stormed from the forecastle. Marco could see Alonso clearly now, and beyond him, Garrido. Garrido grinned.

"You are well, yes?" he called to Marco from the stairs.

Marco's windpipe throbbed, and he was still dizzy. But he nodded.

"Good," grinned Garrido. "I will go above now and save our sorry lives. Alonso, you will join me?"

Alonso looked at Marco. His face was kind. He seemed as though he wanted to say something to the boy. But when he spoke, it was over his shoulder, to Garrido. "Yes, I will join you, Garrido."

"Good!" shouted Garrido, "I would hate for the ship to sink, and for you to be the idiot talking to his young friend as fishes swim by." Garrido clambered back through the door. Alonso chuckled. Then he turned, and in a moment he disappeared through the door himself, gone to battle the storm.

Alone in the forecastle, Marco slid to the floor, breathing deeply. If Alonso knew about the pouch, would he congratulate Marco? Would he smile and slap Marco on the back for being so clever? Marco decided that Alonso need not know about his enterprise. Let Alonso care for his own fortune, thought Marco. He stood unsteadily, and felt under his mattress for the pouch.

———

Somehow the storm ended. Somehow the morning came. Marco opened his eyes and heard the crew on deck. He heard water being pushed over the ship's sides—sloshing back into the sea. He had had fallen asleep on the floor next to his bunk. He climbed to his feet and stretched the soreness out of his limbs. Then, on heavy feet, he walked to the door and out into morning.

The ship glistened with rainwater. Drops of water fell from the spider web of lines that rigged the masts. Men wrung water from their shirts. Bits of seaweed adorned one section of the gunwale. As Marco watched, Alonso and another man gathered it up and plopped it into the gray waves. Marco squinted in the brightness.

A sharp voice sounde. "There he is! The boy who stole from me! *Capitan!*"

Marco looked up, toward the sound of the voice. There, between Marco and the sun, was the unmistakable silhouette of Matanza. The man had stopped in mid-descent from the ratlines, and hung there—his finger pointed like a dagger at Marco.

In an instant, conversations stopped and ropes went slack. The tiller let go of the wheel. All eyes were turned on Marco—Marco, in his bare feet and his dry shirt. Marco's heart began to thump in his chest. In the haze of the morning, he had almost forgotten about the pouch. Marco saw a door open, and into the light strode Captain Herrera.

"What's all this?" said the captain.

Marco opened his mouth to speak, but Matanza spoke more quickly. "During the storm," he shouted, "my pouch somehow left my neck. Through the gale, I saw the boy skulk off with it!"

The captain's eyes fell on Marco. Marco's heart beat faster.

"Boy," said the captain, "you are a guest on this ship. What say you to this?"

Marco looked down at the wooden deck. He was a guest on this ship. The captain's voice had spoken those words clearly. Where would he go if he wore out his welcome? Men were thrown overboard for less. Marco imagined himself falling down into the sea—the black water crushing the breath out of him. He thought of his father—longed for him. Then he thought of showing the gold to Pollito. The captain's gaze was so stern as to will the truth from Marco. Marco felt himself buckling under it. But somewhere—deep inside the part of him that imagined showing the gold to

Pollito—he found the strength to continue the trick. "I don't know what he's talking about," he said, softly.

"He lies!" roared Matanza. He came clambering down the ropes.

"Quiet!" shouted the captain. He looked again at Marco. When he spoke, his voice was quiet, but anger rose in it like water coming to a boil.

"Boy, can you look me in the face and tell me that you did not take Matanza's pouch?"

Marco kept his eyes on the deck. Could he continue the lie if he looked into the captain's eyes? Marco's fortune, he knew, hung in the balance. His mother was dead. His father was lost at sea. In Spain, when he looked for admiration in the eyes of his friends, he saw only pity—even in the eyes of Pollito. Marco was nothing. He had nothing. He thought of the pouch. How might such a sum be spent by a boy—no ... by a man? Marco was sure he had ceased being a boy when he took his fortune into his own hands. When, during the storm, he had shown the sense to seize the opportunity that had presented itself. A man now—no more a boy—thought Marco, with a man's fortune and a man's desire to rise beyond the poor life he'd been born to. Marco the boy might have trembled to look into the eyes of the captain. But Marco the man took a breath, and raised his head. He locked his eyes on the captain's stern face—

looked directly beneath the captain's brows, and spoke.

"Matanza's crazy," he said. "I don't know anything about his stupid pouch."

"Liar!" shouted Matanza. He was on deck now, and he barreled toward Marco. The captain, without looking away from Marco's eyes, held up a hand. Matanza stopped, as if the captain's hand were a wand that had turned him to stone. For a moment, the deck was silent. Not a man spoke. Marco's heart froze in his throat, but he did not look away from the captain's eyes. Matanza clenched and unclenched his fists. His jaw pulsed as he ground his teeth. The captain stood frowning at Marco. The three of them formed a triangle. Outside the triangle stood the door to the forecastle. Finally, the captain spoke.

"Search the boy's things," he said.

The men flew into activity. Matanza bounded through the door and into the darkness. Men followed him. Alonso and Garrido flowed by, borne toward the forecastle like pebbles in a brook. For a moment, Marco remained still, his eyes locked doggedly on the captain's. Then, the captain pointed toward the door. They both turned, and went in.

Marco's eyes adjusted to the darkness of the forecastle. He had never seen so many men in there at once. Between Marco and his bunk stood a gauntlet of wide-eyed sailors. They had crowded into the cramped space to gawk. Marco traded places in his mind with the men he looked at. Were they in his place, would any of them not have taken the pouch where it lay in the storm on the deck last night? *No*, decided Marco. *We are all the same—not because we all took the pouch, but because we would have. Each of us would have.*

Matanza stood by Marco's bunk. He had not waited to begin ransacking Marco's things. Truly, there were almost no things to ransack. Matanza stood facing Marco and the captain, his body tensed like an animal ready to spring. At his feet lay Marco's straw mattress and his wool blanket—everything that Marco had owned, before last night.

"Well?" said the captain.

"The pouch is not here," growled Matanza.

"Not there?" repeated the captain. "But Señor, you were so certain."

"I *am* certain!" cried Matanza. "The boy is guilty! I watched him come down here with the pouch! I followed him!"

"Did you see the pouch itself?" asked the captain.

"The boy's back was turned—his arms drawn up before his chest."

The captain turned to Marco. "Your arms drawn up? You can explain?"

Marco didn't hesitate. "My hands were over my mouth," said Marco. "In the storm, I was afraid I would retch my guts out." Laughter from the other sailors filled the forecastle.

The captain addressed Matanza. "Señor," he said, "If the boy had the pouch, surely you would have found it last night when you followed him here."

"I might have," retorted Matanza, "had not that man drawn me from my search." Matanza pointed a finger at Alonso. This was unexpected. All eyes turned toward the old sailor.

"Señor Alonso," said the captain, "do you know anything of this?"

Alonso shrugged. "I know nothing of Matanza's purse. I followed him here last night because he was angry—bound to waste his energy throttling Marco when we needed him on deck. I have no sympathy for thieves, but I suggested he come back to the boy when we were further from drowning. And you see, he has come, and there is nothing." Alonso shrugged again. "Before those facts, some would call Marco innocent."

Matanza wasn't finished. "Who is to say that you have not planned with the boy?"

Again, Alonso shrugged. "Search my things, then," he said.

"There is no need!" came a voice at the back of the crowd. It was Garrido, who pushed past the sailors.

"*Permiso*. Excuse me. *Disculpeme*," and then, finally arriving at the front of the crowd, "*Capitan*, Alonso was working beside me all night—and beside you too, *Señor*," he nodded toward Matanza. "Alonso could never have hidden the pouch among his things. He hasn't even been to bed yet." He paused. "Señor Matanza, I watched lines and spars swipe at you last night with such force as to fling a pouch from anyone's neck. And you—huddled against the gunwale with the drop to the sea only inches away. *Que Dios me perdone*, but it would seem that your pouch was hurled into the waves by the storm."

Matanza began to protest, "But ... "

"I agree," said Captain Herrera. His eyes were not on Matanza, but on Marco. "The boy's behavior has been beyond reproach. He did not take what was yours, Señor Matanza. We are finished here. All of you, back to your work."

The crowd of men broke up. They flowed back through the forecastle door into the open sun. Some of them chuckled. Some of them patted Marco on the shoulder. Some patted Matanza on the shoulder. For them, it had been a good game—a morning diversion. Marco did not look at Matanza as the man passed, though he felt sure that Matanza was looking at him. Then Matanza spoke, and Marco jumped.

"You know my name, boy?"

"Yes, I know your name," muttered Marco, still looking at the floor.

"Be sure that you keep my name in your mind then," said Matanza. He turned and climbed the stairs back into the soggy morning. Marco shuddered. The name *Matanza* meant *slaughter*.

'A moment later, as Alonso passed Marco, he looked thoughtfully at the boy. Marco felt uncomfortable under the man's gaze.

"You are a good boy, Marco," said the old man. He placed his hand on Marco's head, and then climbed from the hatch. "It is early yet. The captain will not mind, I think, if you went back to your bunk for awhile longer."

Marco had been hoping for just such permission. It had been a long and difficult night. After all, he had spent much of the night lost in thought, before he hid the pouch deep in the bottom of Alonso's sea bag.

Chapter 5

That night, Alonso moved his hammock near to the place where Marco slept. When it was late, he whispered to Marco.

"Garrido is on watch. All else are asleep. Would you like to walk above decks for a moment? We would be unbothered, I think."

Marco ached for fresh air. He was happy to creep with

Alonso up the stairs. His bare feet made almost no noise. Alonso, too, wore no shoes. Soon they were in the cool air of a deep blue night. Loose sailcloth flapped listlessly above them, and the great moon cast the sea in gray. Marco looked up. His mouth fell open. The stars shone, fierce and white. They looked as if they swam in great, silent waves above the ship. *There are no stars like stars at sea,* he thought. I wonder if my father can see such stars tonight. He looked at Alonso. Alonso had spent years at sea, and had seen many night skies over the ocean. But he too was looking up. Gazing at the stars, he wore the same awed expression that Marco had surely worn. *Perhaps,* thought Marco, looking at his friend, *some wonders never grow old.*

Beneath the stars, washed in the cool breeze and the soft sounds of the water, there was silence between the two. Peace. Marco had hardly ever known it in all his short life. Finally, Marco spoke.

"Alonso?"

"Yes, little one?"

"You told me that Juan Ponce would make me a rich man when we got to San Juan."

Alonso turned to Marco. "I said that to cheer you up. I don't know if you will become rich," he said.

"But is that why men leave their homes and go to sea? To become rich? Is that what my father sought?"

"I do not know your father," said Alonso. "But many men seek for riches. San Juan is full of such men. I do not know if Juan Ponce will make you rich, but he has made himself so."

"If he is rich, then why does he wish to go again to sea?" asked Marco.

"I do not know Juan Ponce any better then I know your father," said Alonso. "But they say that riches have not made him happy. And he is surrounded by Columbuses."

"Columbuses?"

"The family of the great discoverer. Christopher Columbus, the father of this New World, has gone. But his son Diego remains on Hispaniola, the island discovered by his father. The king would have made Juan Ponce governor of all those new lands I think, but Diego grabs and grabs at what his father discovered. It is his right, under the law. They are not good neighbors, he and Juan Ponce. So Juan Ponce prepares to go away. But there is more."

"More?"

"You will laugh," said Alonso, "because you are already young."

"Already? You mean 'still young,' not 'already young,' I think," corrected Marco.

"Maybe," Alonso shrugged. "But word has reached Spain of a singular place of water—natives in the New

World speak of it—a place of water in which an old man can bathe and become forever young and strong. Some say Juan Ponce will find it."

Marco laughed. "A good tale," he said.

Alonso shrugged again. "I told you that you would laugh," he said, "because you are already young." Alonso was silent again, and looked out to sea. For the first time since Marco had known him, his face seemed old and sad.

Marco did not ask anything else of Alonso. They stood together in the night for a long moment. From high above them, Garrido hooted softly. Marco and Alonso looked up to find him grinning down at them and waving. They waved back. Then they turned for the door again.

His hand on the latch, Alonso stiffened. Like lightning, his hand pushed back on Marco's chest. Marco dropped into shadow behind his friend. At first, the night seemed as quiet as ever. Then, Marco heard it. A soft shuffling—no louder than cloth tumbled against cloth. Seconds later came the sifting sound of a straw mattress being moved about. Someone was awake in the forecastle, and the sounds were coming from the direction of Marco's bed. There was no lantern light to accompany the sounds—only darkness. Alonso turned quietly to Marco, and leaned his long head down near the boy's.

"I'm going in there," he whispered, so softly that Marco

wondered if he'd heard correctly.

"You can't! He might—"

"If that's Matanza, whatever he wishes to do he wishes to do to you, not to me," interrupted Alonso. "I am a free man aboard this ship. You must hide here."

"Alone?"

"Marco, the rascal is rummaging under your bed. I go to stop him, yes?" Alonso pushed Marco into the shadow of the mast, and Marco crouched behind it, his heart beating.

Alonso slipped into the darkness and down the stairs. Marco strained his ears to hear. There were whispers between the men. Marco heard Matanza say words like "sneak," and "rat," and then only whispers again. With each scattered word that Marco understood, his heart jumped. Finally, he heard more. It was the voice of Alonso, and it did not whisper. "Fine, then," it said. "You would search the deck and speak with the boy? Be my guest."

Alonso's full, strong voice was all the warning Marco needed. He felt panic rise in his brain. Matanza would come to the deck, and he would find Marco cowering behind the mast. It was a poor hiding place. Marco searched with his eyes for a better one. He could hear Matanza moving toward the forecastle door. Then, in an instant, Marco scurried across the deck toward the gunwale. When he got there, he placed his hands firmly on the rail, and launched himself over the side. He heard Garrido yelp from the crow's nest. But Marco was not so desperate as to abandon ship. He held to the pegs that secured lines to the gunwale, and hung over the ocean, pressed tight against the hull of the ship.

In an instant, he regretted his move. Here, he could neither see Matanza nor hear his bare feet on deck. The ocean was below him, and a silent enemy above. Fear rose cold in Marco's heart. His only comfort came from Garrido. If Marco craned his neck, he could see his friend high in the crow's nest.

Matanza spoke.

"You, Garrido! You hollered!" he said.

"Pinched myself awake is all I did," cooed Garrido.

"Hard enough to make you yelp in pain?" Matanza's voice was doubtful.

"I was very sleepy," shrugged Garrido.

Matanza was silent. Then he spoke again.

"Have you seen the boy on deck tonight?"

"Is the boy mine to keep?" grumbled Garrido. "Check his bunk. He's been there for days."

"Are you sure you haven't—"

"Look, Señor," interrupted Garrido. "If my work tonight were watching what happens on deck, I would be down there on deck. As it happens, my work tonight is to watch the sea. And the boy is not on the sea."

Matanza muttered something under his breath. Then all was quiet. Marco hung until his arms ached. Surely, Matanza had given up. Marco convinced himself of it. He pulled himself quietly up, inch by inch. When his eyes were above the rail, his blood froze. Matanza, his back toward Marco, stood not three feet away from Marco's hiding place. Marco gasped, and dropped below the rail. He heard a scuffling as Matanza whirled. The man had heard him! Marco bit his lip, and waited for discovery. Then, another sound made his heart jump. Something clattered on the far side of the deck.

"You heard that?" from Matanza.

"Eh?" from Garrido.

Silence.

Silence.

Then, from far away, Matanza's voice again.

"You threw a loaf of bread?" The voice was far away—the opposite end of the deck from Marco's hiding place.

Garrido spoke, "Had I a loaf of bread up here, I would keep it for my supper," he said.

"It looks as if someone hurled this loaf of bread, and knocked this lantern over," said Matanza.

Nothing but a shrug from Garrido.

"It is lucky that the lantern was not lit."

Nothing but a shrug from Garrido.

Silence.

Silence.

Footsteps, crossing the deck and fading away.

Marco's hands throbbed. Finally, in a loud whisper from the crow's nest, he heard his friend.

"You are a very dangerous boy, and you may come up now from your very foolish hiding place. Also, you owe me a loaf of bread."

Marco looked up. Even from far away, and even at night, Marco could see Garrido's grin.

Chapter 6

Marco's arms still ached when he awoke. The sun streamed through the openings in the forecastle. Across the forecastle, a dark shape sat still, looking at him. He knew it was Matanza. Marco flailed out his arm and found Garrido's shoulder. His friend was asleep on a stool next to Marco's bunk. Garrido grunted awake. "Good morning, boy," he said. He looked off toward the shadowy shape.

"Good morning, Señor Matanza," he said.

Sailors rolled from their beds, and the forecastle was a zoo of stretching, scratching, and yawning. Matanza remained still. Garrido remained next to Marco.

Suddenly, a voice: "Land! Land ho! *Tierra seca!*"

The men jolted from their weariness. Half-dressed, they swarmed above-decks. Garrido swept Marco along with them, safe in the crook of his arm. Only then did Matanza move, climbing the stairs along with everyone else. In the distance, long and low on the horizon, was San Juan Bautista. Men grinned and slapped each other on the back. One man threw a hat into the air, and everyone laughed when it went into the ocean. Joking and singing, the crew began preparing the ship for port. Hope rose in Marco's heart. Then he remembered his enemy, and with a start realized that he could not see Matanza. Frantically he looked about, and grasped Garrido's hand. Finally, he saw the man—up in the rigging, yanking on one line or another. He was at work with the rest of the crew, and, for a while at least, Matanza would not spring out at Marco from behind a barrel.

In preparation for their arrival in San Juan, Marco joined Alonso and his detail, counting crates—moving many of them up onto deck for easy unloading. In the bustle, no one saw Marco reach deep into Alonso's sea bag and withdraw Matanza's pouch—no one, that is, until he was putting the bag back where he found it.

"Looks like my sea bag," said Alonso from behind him. Marco jumped.

"Er ... indeed it is," the boy stammered. "I thought ... I thought I would carry it above for you."

Alonso held out a hand. "Give the bag here," he said. "We'll leave the personals for later—after the cargo has gone off, yes?"

Alonso took the bag from Marco. As he hefted it, a quizzical look came over his face. He looked for a long moment at Marco. Something seemed to have dawned on the old man. Marco found it difficult to look back. At last, Alonso put his sea bag down again. "You cart some of the smaller casks above decks, eh?" he pointed, and Marco quickly rushed toward the hold. Alonso's gaze had felt like a trap, and Marco was happy to escape into work. He made trip after trip from the hold up to the main deck. He stacked his cargo against the rail. Each new load was another opportunity to look out over the approaching dock. One trip, and he could see the dock in the distance. Two more, and they had reached land. Another, and the gangplank was down. A man with a graying beard stood at the end of it. The man spoke in shouts to Captain Herrera, who spoke in shouts to the crew. Some crew tied off the shrouds. Others left their sea jobs to carry barrels and boxes down the gangplank. As the work of being at sea came to a close, the work of bringing everyone ashore began. The gray-bearded man watched from the dock, shouting directions from time to time. Other men, not from the crew of *La Juana*, joined the effort. In a flash, it seemed, the big ship was emptied of her cargo. Men now dug through corners, withdrawing their personal things. Forgotten shirts, bits of candle, and single stockings littered the forecastle.

Marco had the pouch safely hung around his neck—tucked down beneath his shirt. His adventure with Matanza was nearly over. He had come to the New World, and he had come to it a rich man. Only a few moments more and the crew would separate for taverns and inns. Marco would soon be safe, lost in the streets of San Juan with a pouch of gold. Even now, some men were shaking hands or swapping the details of future commissions. Captain Herrera was on the gangplank, speaking with the gray-bearded man. Marco could not hear them, but at the end of their conversation, a large and heavy box was given into Herrera's hands. Herrera passed the box to the ship's paymaster. Men crowded around the paymaster as he came aboard ship again. Marco stood apart from them. Inside the knot of sailors, Marco heard the jingling of coins and the shouting of names. Everyone, it seemed, was eager to gather around where the paymaster sat. Everyone, that is, except for the two members of the voyage that could expect no pay from it—the two members of the voyage that had come aboard in the middle, and not as hired hands: Marco and Matanza.

Marco stood near the gangplank, hoping only to say farewell to his friends and be on his way. Matanza sat on the gunwale opposite the boy, at the other end of the deck. He sat exactly as Marco had first seen him on the pirate ship. His eyes, now as then, were on Marco. But then, Marco had been a frightened captive. Now, he was free—the master of his own fortune in a New World. Marco shrugged his shoulders at Matanza.

And the cord round his neck snapped.

With a dull thud, the pouch slipped through Marco's shirt and onto the deck. The impact knocked two gold coins up through the gathered mouth of the pouch. The coins caught the sun for a moment, and then rang in harmony on the deck. The crew turned.

Matanza's eyes went wide. His mouth opened, too surprised to speak or shout—but not too surprised to pounce. Marco braced himself for a blow. But between Matanza and Marco were two split seconds. In the first, Matanza—thinking perhaps that guilt would hold Marco for a moment—bent to snatch up the loose coins.

In the second, Marco scooped up the pouch and ran for his life.

Behind him, Marco heard a great shout go up from the crew. Some of them laughed. Marco did not turn around. In his mind's eye he saw Alonso, who had defended him when Matanza had searched his things. Marco did not turn around. He imagined the face of Garrido, who had kept him safe during Matanza's midnight prowl on the deck of *La Juana*. Marco did not turn around.

Boots clattered on the gangplank behind Marco. Matanza was chasing him. Marco plunged into the crowd on the dock. Chickens squawked and scattered. Bundles of goods were upset as Marco muscled his way past. A great yellow cloud of saffron dust poofed up behind Marco as he toppled precious packets of spices—spices that had come safely across thousands of miles of ocean, and now lay scattered in the dusty street. Men's fortunes spoiled as a ten-year-old flailed past. Shouts went up. Men shook fists. And now it was more than Matanza behind him. A little knot of merchants and dockworkers followed him like a cloud of hornets. Marco clutched the purse and slipped through the tangles of adult legs, cart wheels, and rickety merchant stands. Wooden patios and mud buildings lined the wharf. Around them and between them Marco darted like a rabbit. His pursuers clamored after, calling ahead of them for help. Blessedly, no hand reached out to stop Marco.

By now, Marco's breath came in ragged gasps. He still had them by fifty yards, but soon Matanza and the others would catch him. He was sure of it. As he passed building after building, snatches of laughter and talk floated out of doorways. Then, Marco passed a silent door. No laughter came from it. As far as Marco could tell in the split second as he passed it, it was an empty building. Marco stopped in his tracks, then darted through the doorway. Against one inside wall of the building was a desk. There was an inkpot and a rack filled with paper. There were a few chairs pushed beneath a wooden table. The table sat against a wall. Above the table was a window.

"He went into the scribe's!" The voice was distant, but it made Marco's heart leap. Without a thought, Marco scampered up onto the table, and then to the windowsill. Marco glanced at the ground. Only a few feet. He could jump to the ground without any problem. But as he stood, something tickled his neck. His head jerked upward. The roof of the quiet room was made of straw, bundled together and lashed to joists that ran the length of the building. Stray straws hung down in front of the window. As Marco looked up, they brushed his cheek. A moment ago they had tickled his neck. Standing on the sill, Marco reached outside the building and up, as far as he could on the roof. He pulled at a handful of straw. It held fast.

"Through the doorway! We've got him!" someone shouted. Marco put the loose mouth of the pouch in his teeth. He glanced toward the door, then reached out and up again, gripping the straw of the roof in his fists. He swung his legs out the window, and scrabbled up the wall, pulling with his arms. Mud kicked away from the wall as he climbed. But in a moment, he was up. He lay flat against the straw. Below him, the sound of hurried feet filled the empty building.

And voices.

"What, you! He's not in here!"

"Quiet! I saw him enter this doorway not ten seconds ago!"

"Look in that cupboard!"

Then, Marco heard more feet, and another voice.

"*Què Diablos!* What are you men doing in my shop! A man goes for bread and drink, and comes back to find the world going through his things! What's all this?"

"Why don't you lock your door!" snarled one of Marco's pursuers.

"Why would anyone rob me? What would anyone do with pens, ink, and paper? What would you do? Can you read?"

Silence.

"Write?"

Silence.

"There then. Tell me how to run my own shop. Get out, the lot of you."

Someone else spoke. Marco thought it might be Matanza.

"A boy ran in here to hide. He stole from me—"

"—And ruined a bolt of my cloth," said another voice.

"And upset a month's worth of spice goods," said another.

"And?" said the owner. "You think I'm hiding him here beneath my shirt? If I were a boy on the run and happened in here, I'd be out that window, I would."

There was but a half-second of silence, and then more shouting and the shuffling of boots.

"Out the window he's gone!"

"After him, and search as you go!"

Marco lay flat against the roof. Soon, the voices of his pursuers faded into the general noise of the crowd. Cautiously, he sat up and made ready to lower himself down over the lip of the roof. He chose an edge of the roof far from the window. He'd drop from the roof, and with his pouch of money disappear into the streets of San Juan. He braced himself for the slow crawl to the roof's edge.

Carefully, he pushed against the roof, putting his weight on his right palm as he held the pouch in his left.

Marco put his right arm squarely through the roof.

"What's this!" a yell went up from inside. Like lightning, something gripped Marco's hand. Marco screamed. The vice gripped harder—and pulled. One swift, steady pull, and Marco tumbled through the straw roof. With a howl, he tumbled all the way to the floor. Only after he'd landed, bruised and frightened, did the man let go of his hand. Startled, still clutching the pouch, Marco looked up at the man. He was a great, round, red-faced fellow. He held a fine coat in his hand. A halo of red hair shone in the sunlight streaming through the fresh hole in the roof. Bits of straw floated down around him. The man took a deep breath, pointed his great finger at Marco's head, and opened his mouth to speak.

And Marco bolted.

Right between the man's legs he scuttled, and out the door—back through the street, further and further from the dock he ran, away from Matanza, away from the merchants, and away from the great, red-haired scribe, who even now shouted after him.

"Curse you, rabbit!" came the yell. "Look at the size of me! Do you think I can run you down and carry my belly at the same time? Get back here!"

Chapter 7

So this is the country of Juan Ponce, where men go to get rich. Marco bounced the pouch in his hand. It was still full of coins, and Marco was hungry. It was time to find the market.

Food wasn't difficult to find. He had only to retrace his steps back toward the wharf. Escaping from Matanza, he had passed stall after stall of fresh fruits and vegetables, and more than one alehouse.

But it wasn't just finding food. Marco was only an hour old in the New World, and already he had enemies. He had outrun them once, but only by luck. The merchants whose goods he'd ruined might not recognize him again—from the front. But Matanza—Matanza was different. Thinking about Matanza, the pouch of gold felt heavy in Marco's hand. On his way to the wharf markets, Marco peered around each corner before rounding it, and moved across open spaces quickly, seeking the safety of crowds.

Finally, the street opened onto the wide waterfront. In every direction, people bustled from stall to stall. Men pulled fish off of boats or loaded nets onto them. Carts loaded with vegetables ranged before Marco, and his stomach growled. Marco forgot his caution then. It was good to be in San Juan, and it was good to be rich. Marco pulled open the mouth of the pouch, and fingered the coins inside. He stepped up to a stall filled with mangos. The seller attended to a large woman, who took the fruits one by one in her hand. She tapped them, and squeezed them, and put most of them back. All the time, the woman spoke loudly to the stall's owner. They argued and shrugged and argued more, and finally the woman trundled off, with her hands full of fruit. Marco was next. But the merchant instead waved Marco aside, and turned his attention to another woman, a woman that stood behind Marco. *Coming from weeks at sea, and after a good run and a fall through a roof, I must not look like a rich man,* Marco thought. But whether his clothes were fine or not, the gold, he felt sure, would speak for him. He held the pouch up, and jingled it loudly.

Marco felt a hand on his shoulder. He pulled the bag of gold tightly against his chest. He wheeled around, even as he yelped, "Matanza!" His heart leaped into his throat. Instinctively, he looked up for the adult face that must belong to the hand—the scowling, bearded face of Matanza. But he saw no one. He lowered his eyes.

There, before him, stood a girl.

She was dressed in a dirty shirt and boys' trousers. Her feet were bare. Her hair hung in tangles about her face. She looked to be about Marco's age. Even now, her hand was raised, as if to rest on Marco's shoulder.

"What do you want?" asked Marco, his pulse slowing.

"*Ven aqui!*" the girl said. She motioned to Marco with her raised hand. "Come!"

Marco hesitated.

"Come on, *vago,*" said the girl. Marco glanced back at the stall. The merchant still argued with his female customer. Marco was nervous, but he hadn't had a conversation with anyone his own age in weeks. He followed the ragged girl around a quiet corner. She was stealthy—agile like a cat. When they reached the shadow of the corner, the girl rolled her clear eyes.

"*Estàs Loco?*" said the girl. "A pouch of money like that. It's a good way to get killed on the wharf—a kid in a ragged shirt and bare feet, with a sack of *dinero*. You wouldn't last twenty seconds," said the girl in the ragged shirt and bare feet. She looked at Marco. "Where did you steal it?" she asked.

"I didn't steal it," Marco lied. The girl shrugged.

"Suit yourself," she said. "But don't spend it here. Don't pay for your food like an idiot."

"Watch who you call an idiot."

"Only an idiot would use gold like that to buy food when there's plenty of food to be had for free—*gratis*," said the girl.

"What do you mean," said Marco.

"Follow me," said the girl with a jerk of her head. Then she ran.

Marco looked back at the vegetable stall for a moment. The merchant was arguing with another customer. Then Marco turned to follow the girl.

Through streets she led him, and then into wide spaces—fields on either side of the broad road. She ran easily and quickly on the hard dirt. Marco, however, began to tire. The girl was pulling steadily ahead of him. Finally, Marco called out:

"*Espera*! Wait!" he gasped. The girl turned. She looked at Marco and laughed. But she waited.

"What did you mean by 'Matanza,'?" asked the girl.

"What?" said Marco.

"'Matanza.' You said 'Matanza' when I tapped you on the shoulder in the market."

"Matanza is the name of the ... " Marco stopped short.

"Name of the what?" asked the girl.

"The name of the former owner of this purse," said Marco.

"And, of course, you didn't steal it."

Marco shrugged.

"What sort of man is he?" continuedJuanita.

"A sailor, looking for glory in the New World—looking beyond San Juan, I imagine," said Marco.

"Where is Matanza now?"asked Juanita.

"Who knows? He was on the wharf last time I saw him."

Juanita thought for a moment. "Matanza is not a common name," she said.

"More common now than yesterday," said Marco. "He made enough of a fuss on the wharf today to make him a famous man."

Juanita did not respond.

"Where are we going?" complained Marco, changing the subject.

The girl pointed. "There," she said.

Ahead of them was a great grey house. It was made of adobe, and set back from the road. In San Juan, where most of the buildings were small structures made of mud and straw, the house looked like a fortress. Fine carriages and horses lined the road facing the house. Dark-skinned men held the reins of some of the horses, and tended the carriages.

"What place is this?" asked Marco.

"You are new to San Juan," said the girl. This is the home of Juan Ponce—"

"—Juan Ponce? From Leon, in Spain?" asked Marco. His eyes went wide.

"I don't know where he's from. Probably you are right and he's from Spain, like everybody else. But he came here from Santo Domingo, the other great island, where he had an even greater home—all of stone. He's an Indian killer. And he's rich. Today he's having a party."

"A party?" asked Marco.

"A wedding," said the girl. "A wedding for some fat soldier's daughter. There will be food. So much food that they will throw away to the pigs as much as they eat at the table." She turned to Marco, wrinkled up her nose, and made the snorting sound of a pig. Marco laughed.

"So how do we get it?" Marco asked.

"We wait until the wedding is over, and then, when the guests are gone, we run among the servants and take what we can. We will only have a moment, enough to run the length of the party and grab what our hands can carry." She looked at Marco. "My hands can carry a lot," she added.

They were close to the house now. They had caught the eyes of some of the dark-skinned men who tended the animals and carriages.

"Who are they?" asked Marco.

"They are Taino," said the girl. "This was their island before people like us came from Santo Domingo next door and from across the ocean in Spain."

Marco looked at the girl. She shrugged.

"Now it's our island," she said with a grin. "The Taino tend the horses and till the fields and mine Juan Ponce's gold."

Juan Ponce's gold, thought Marco. "I thought Juan Ponce killed Indians," he said.

The girl shrugged again. "Not Taino. Not now. Now he just kills Caribs."

They were among the carriages now. The house loomed.

Even from the road, Marco could hear the noises of a feast. Sometimes a great laugh would rise from the direction of the house. Sometimes cheers. Marco and his companion were silent for a while.

Finally, Marco said, "What is your name?"

"I am Juana. Little Juana—Juanita," said the girl.

Marco stifled a laugh.

"My name is funny?" asked the girl. She made a fist. Marco cowered.

"No. No. Not funny at all," he managed. "It is only that I have spent the last many weeks with a Juana." The girl— Juanita—looked quizzically at him.

"It was the name of the ship that brought me here," explained Marco.

"A ship? I see," said Juanita. If she wanted more explanation, she didn't ask for it. There was silence again, while Marco tried to keep from laughing. Then he snorted.

"What!" said Juanita.

"We called the ship *La Loca*," he explained.

Juanita slugged him in the gut. Marco doubled over. "Very funny," she said.

When Marco could breathe again, he spoke.

"How long must we wait?" he asked.

"To eat? Until the wedding meal is finished," said Juanita. "Are you hungry or bored?"

"Both," said Marco.

"I could punch you again. That wouldn't be boring," said Juanita.

"No, thanks," muttered Marco.

Juanita looked at Marco. His hands were over his stomach. She rolled her eyes.

"Come on, then, let's go take a look at the wedding," she said, without smiling. Then she trotted toward the house. Marco scrambled after her.

Juanita headed straight for the corner of the house, far from the front door. Marco followed. She led him along the side of the house, and turned the corner again. They were at the rear of the house now, the side that faced away from the road and onto Juan Ponce's land. It was a lovely, warm day. The windows and doors along the back of the house stood open, and a few servants in shirtsleeves stood talking near the doors. Perhaps the servants did not see Marco and Juanita. Perhaps they saw them but took no notice. In any case, Marco and Juanita found a spot in the shade of a shrub. The voices inside the house rang out clearly through the open windows. Marco listened.

"...yes, yes, if you care for that sort of thing," he heard. "But Juan Ponce's skills lie elsewhere now. If he wishes to go to sea again, let him do it in his dreams!" There was laughter, and the laughter encouraged the speaker. "In real life, we need him here. Juan Ponce, scourge of the Caribs! Were he to leave—well, with what would we scourge the Caribs then?" Laugher, and the voice rose even higher— "With what, Juan Ponce? What say you who would so willingly leave us alone on San Juan?" There was more laughter, and banging on glass, and shouts of "Yes, yes!" and "What say you! What say you indeed!"

They're heckling him into giving a speech, thought Marco.

Finally, the shouts erupted into cheers, followed by laughter, then silence. Then a second voice spoke alone.

"It is at times like these that one regrets opening his doors to his many friends," said the voice. The house roared with laughter. The second voice went on.

"I welcome you here, and you drink my wine, and you sit yourselves down on my fine chairs, and you track the dust of your feet on my fine floors, and then you've the gall to call me names." More laughter.

"The next time you wish to marry off a daughter," said the voice, "you'll please have the kindness to marry her off in your own home!" Laughter. Then the first voice spoke again.

"Alas, my Cynthia is the last to marry—and marry well, I hope. Do you hear that, groom?" There was a banging sound, like a stick on a table, and more laughter. The voice continued.

"Yes, Juan Ponce, you and I are both alone now."

A third voice spoke. "Then perhaps you marry each other!" The house fairly split with laughter. After a long time, the laughter died, and the second voice, the voice of Juan Ponce, spoke again.

"Yes, alone. I've given the last of my daughters over to a good man," said Juan Ponce.

"And made that man governor of San Juan!" someone said. Laughter.

"Yes, yes. He was Governor of San Juan for a while," said Juan Ponce.

"And time has marched on," continued the first voice, "and you have taken a good, long trip to Spain for heaven-knows-what. Now you are back—with plenty of time on your hands to keep the Caribs at bay. They continue to attack our settlements—to kill off our Taino. You defended us before, Juan Ponce, with your wife and children hanging onto the tail of your horse. And now, after Leonor's death—God rest her soul—you, you have time to stretch your arm against the Caribs, unfettered by your family—"

"Hold, friend," interrupted Juan Ponce, not unkindly. "When you speak so of Leonor and the children, you speak within one step of speaking too far." Silence from inside the house. Then, Juan Ponce spoke again. "The fetters of which you speak—I long to still be tied by them. My house is empty, and it is time to put down my sword and leave the scourging of the Caribs to—" (and here Juan Ponce cleared his throat) "—better men." There was laughter from some, and Juan Ponce continued. "Time," he said, "to turn my prow again toward the colonization of *La Florida* and the search for Bimini—"

"—Bimini?" the first voice interrupted. "The mythical island full of gold and running with magic water? Myths! Described to you a decade ago by Tainos that were likely drunk. It doesn't exist, old friend. You go to chase a mirage if you go to chase Bimini."

Juan Ponce continued, "Well, to colonize *La Florida* then."

The first voice would not keep silent. "*And* to search for Bimini," it said. "Don't pretend you didn't say it, Juan Ponce. You go to drink from a fountain of eternal youth—a fountain that exists only in your head."

"In any case, I go," said Juan Ponce. "Even today, I went to the wharf to oversee the arrival of a supply ship, laden with goods for my journey. The wheels are turning, friends, and they will bear me away from here within a week."

Supply ship? Even today? A question lodged itself in Marco's mind, and his ears weren't tools enough to answer it. He set his pouch on the ground, and pushed himself slowly up the wall where he and Juanita listened. Slowly, his curiosity drew his forehead up over the sill of the window. Inside the large room, men and women sat at tables piled with half-finished food. A bride and groom sat at a long table that stretched the length of the far wall. The eyes of the crowd, like Marco's own, were fixed on a man at the head of the room. The man was on his feet, a glass in his hand. On the man's face was a gray beard. It was the same face and the same beard that belonged to the man who had watched Marco and the others unload *La Juana*. It was the same face that had given the pay box over to Captain Herrera. In an instant, the eyes in that face flicked over to the window where Marco watched. For a moment, the eyes of Marco the orphan met the eyes of Juan Ponce de Leon—the slave trader, the gold miner, the fountain-hunter ... the scourge of the Caribs.

Marco dropped to the ground. "He saw me, Juanita!" he panted. "Juan Ponce saw me. What do we do?"

But Marco's question was met only with silence. Marco was alone. He looked frantically about. Then he stared at the ground. Juanita wasn't there anymore. She had disappeared—and with her, Matanza's pouch.

Chapter 8

The New World is just like the old world, thought Marco. He sat in the shadow where two mossy walls made a dank corner. His dark hair hung loosely before his eyes. His bony arms were folded across his ribs.

It had been six days since Juanita had tricked Marco. Six days since he had looked Juan Ponce de Leon in the eye. Six days since his wild run from Matanza through the streets of San Juan. Now, Marco picked through cast-off food to fill his stomach—just like in Spain. But here, there was no Pollito. No fat Señor Galdame to grin at him and offer him a ladle of milk. No, Marco thought, the New World is not at all like the old world. In the New World, I am alone.

Marco sighed. He was hungry.

He lifted himself to his feet, and looked up and down the street. For six days, he had looked up and down the street each time he walked out into it. He looked for Matanza. He looked for Juanita. Nothing.

Marco crossed the street and headed down it, toward the docks. The sounds and smells of the wharf drifted in around him. He passed carts of vegetables and fish. Cart after cart, it seemed, hosted too few customers to distract a seller long enough for a boy to snatch an apple or a banana. Marco's stomach began to growl.

Then, just ahead of him, he saw a knot of people—men, mostly—gathered around something Marco could not see. *In the middle of that group*, thought Marco, *is a seller attending to a crowd.* Whatever it was he was selling, Marco was sure he could get some without being noticed. He approached the group, elbowing his way between knees and belts. In a moment, he was in the midst of the men.

Sure enough, at the center of the crowd was a cart piled

high with cassava roots. A vegetable-seller stood behind the cart with his arms folded. But the crowd wasn't interested in cassava roots. Perched on the edge of the vegetable cart was an old man. His bare feet swung below him. Wet leather boots lay on the ground at the foot of the cart. Next to the boots, a soaked sea bag sprawled open. The man's clothes hung, damp, around him. And he laughed.

"...could have been worse, I suppose," he said. "'stead of falling off the gangplank in the New World I could have sailed last year with Panfilo de Narvaez!"

"What do you mean?" asked someone in the crowd.

"What do I mean?" asked the old man. "What do I mean?" He pointed in the direction of the voice that had spoken. "What piglet doesn't know of Cortes, sweeping up through the jungles of the New World with his big sword? Why, here you are—in the New World—and you don't know it!" More water came out of his sock. He muttered under his breath. "Gold on the ground right where you can pick it up, and the country full of idiots," he said.

The men around him laughed. The old man laughed too.

"Do you really not know?" he asked. "King Charles sends the mighty Conquistador, the terrible Hernan Cortes, to build a nice little colony in America. Bring back gold from America for the glory of the crown, he surely will. And off goes Cortes. Two years ago he does this. You must know this, yes?"

Some men nodded.

"Perhaps Cortes will find a city of gold" said one man, "and we will go and live there!"

More laughter from the crowd.

"Go and live there, then, and maybe Cortes will eat you for lunch!" said the old man. "Cortes wanders into a village in his shiny armor, and the poor naturals look up and see him all white and shining and say, 'Surely, this is the God of the Sun.' And Cortes, do you think he says 'No, you must be mistaken. It is only I, the mighty Cortes'? No, Cortes polishes up his armor and says, 'Yes, thank you for noticing. Now give me all your gold.'

Marco laughed. The old man went on.

"The king, he now has the God of the Sun on the loose in the New World! You think he likes this?"

Now everyone laughed.

"You laugh!" said the old man. "But the king, he does not laugh. The king sends Panfilo de Narvaez, along with an army and a message for Cortes: that even the God of the Sun still kneels before the Spanish crown. Only last year this happens. And does the God of the Sun say, 'Of course, thank you, King, for reminding me'?

"Tell us!" said someone in the crowd.

The old man grinned a toothless grin. "No! The God of the Sun takes the armies of Narvaez, and gobbles them up!"

"Gobbles them up?" Marco couldn't help himself.

"Yes, rat. He gobbles them up. Takes them away from Narvaez and makes them his own soldiers. And he puts Narvaez in a cage. Even now, Panfilo de Narvaez sits among the natives in a cage, and Cortes cuts with an even bigger sword. Maybe the biggest sword in the world."

The old man pulled on one long sock, and then the other.

"And so you see, it could be worse! It would have been as easy for me to be on Narvaez's ship as on the one that brought me here. But I don't have to tramp through the jungles with the God of the Sun. Yes, I fell off the gangplank when I came, but in an hour I am dry again, in the land of Columbuses—the island of Juan Ponce de Leon, who, like me, wishes to grow old among the pine fruit and the cassava roots."

The old man pulled on one long boot, and then the other. They squished and dripped water.

"Have you not heard?" asked someone in the crowd. "Juan Ponce sails even tomorrow for more adventures beyond *La Florida*!"

"What do you mean?" asked the old man.

"What do I mean? What do I mean?" asked the man

that had spoken.

The crowd laughed.

"What piglet doesn't know that?" shouted someone else.

The crowd roared.

The old man cursed under his breath, dismounted the cassava cart, and picked up his sea bag. He shuffled off to the laughter of the men. The crowd began to break up. Some men stayed to buy cassava roots.

And then Marco saw it.

A tall man stood with his back turned to Marco. He was filling a bag with cassava roots from the cart. Over the man's shoulder was a leather pocket. From the mouth of the pocket peeked something that made Marco's eyes dance.

A purse.

It sat, fat with coins, inside the pocket. The purse dangled before hungry Marco. In Spain, hunger would have driven him to Pollito's house. Pollito's mother would have given him bread and milk.

Marco grabbed the purse. Silently, he slipped it from the pouch. This was not Spain, and there was no Pollito.

Pollito.

Marco imagined the face of his friend. He imagined going back to Spain with a great sack of coins. He imagined holding out his hand to Pollito—and he imagined the conversation they would have.

In his imagination, Pollito said, "Marco! Where did you get such a sack of coins!"

And then, in his imagination, Marco replied, "I went to the New World! I made my fortune there! See, I am a man now!"

This is what Marco tried to make himself say in his imaginary conversation with Pollito. But his imagination would not obey him. Instead, in his imagination, Marco looked away from Pollito and stammered, "I stole these coins, purse by purse, between here and the New World."

And Pollito asked, "Stole them? Why would you steal them?"

In his imagination, Marco paused. Here—in the New World—he was about to steal a purse because he was hungry. But to tell Pollito that hunger had driven him to steal would be a lie. Now he was hungry. But first he had stolen Matanza's purse. He had stolen it when his belly was full—when he had friends around him. He had stolen it because he wanted the money.

In his imagination, Pollito waited for an answer.

In his imagination, Marco could not think of an answer he liked.

In real life, Marco did something that didn't feel like an

answer. But with Pollito staring at him from the back of his brain, it was all he could do.

Marco tugged at the man's shirttail. He held out the purse. "*Señor*, you dropped ... "

The man turned. A large, long face looked down on Marco. Above the face was a tangle of grey hair. A wide smile spread across the face.

"A-Alonso!" shouted Marco.

"Boy." Alonso's grin seemed to grow even wider.

Marco blinked. "Your purse," he said. "You dropped ... "

"Funny that I, who have never dropped a purse in my life, should drop a purse just now—right next to the boy who, by coincidence, did not at all steal Matanza's gold and hide it cleverly in the sea bag of his dirty, smelly friend, thinking that surely his dirty, smelly friend would never rummage in his bag for a clean shirt."

Marco opened his mouth, but could not speak.

"Or at least," said Alonso, "I thought for a moment that you were that boy. But surely that boy would have taken my purse and run off with it, toppling spice jars and hurling silks into the dust behind him."

Marco still could not speak.

Alonso continued. He said his words slowly and carefully, and put his face close to Marco's. "You are clearly some other boy. I am pleased to meet you. My name, as you seem for some mysterious reason to know, is Jerèz. Alonso Martin de Jerèz."

Alonso extended his hand.

Marco's mouth hung open. Still, he was silent.

"Perhaps what you mean to say," said Alonso, "is that it is good to see me, too."

———

Marco sat with Alonso at an inn table. A server brought a platter of meat and two mugs of ale. Alonso looked sheepish.

"I am sorry," said Alonso. "I do not know what children drink. Likely not this." He picked up Marco's mug and moved it next to his own. "Eat, eat," he said.

Marco began to eat, and did not stop as Alonso spoke.

"Some of us—me, Garrido, others, have done it. We will be members of Juan Ponce's crew."

"On his journey to *La Florida*?" asked Marco, his mouth full.

"Look at you, and your '*La Florida*.' I cannot tell you anything, can I? You know about *La Florida*, then. This is good. It prepares the way for my next question."

Marco swallowed. "What is that?"

Alonso finished his mug of ale, and started on Marco's.

"I knew a boy once—about your age—who was brave at sea. He stole from the other men on the ship, though. Of a boy like that, I have nothing to ask." Alonso paused. "But the boy that I am now eating this fine meal with—I might ask if he would like to leave the dusty streets of San Juan and help me count cows and seedlings and plow bits on Juan Ponce's ship with his friend, Alonso."

Marco stopped eating. He stared at Alonso.

"I don't understand ... "

Alonso fidgeted. "What I am asking," he said, "is if you would like to come with me on the sea again, to look for the magic fountain with Juan Ponce."

"The magic fountain? The fountain of eternal youth?"

"If it exists, and if Juan Ponce goes to find it, I would like to find it with him. You will come, yes?"

Marco hesitated.

Alonso spoke again, "Come now, Marco, if I drink from the magic fountain and become a boy again, who will I play with if you do not come?"

Marco grinned. "Yes, Alonso, I will come."

"Good!" said Alonso. "Tomorrow we leave. I found you just in time, no? And a good thing, too. I have a special job for you on this trip. I'll tell you tomorrow, yes? Now we must go—to buy paper and ink for me to count things with."

Alonso and Marco left the inn and walked through the crowded street. They passed door after door. Finally, they stopped at a door in the wall of a small adobe building. Atop the building was a roof of thatched straw. Something caught in Marco's throat. He knew this place.

"I will wait outside," said Marco, urgently.

"Nonsense," said Alonso. "You will enjoy seeing what is in this place: all manner of paper—and a man who writes for sailors who don't know how." He took Marco by the hand and led him through the door. Before them at a familiar table sat a familiar large man with a familiar halo of red hair. He looked at Alonso and smiled. Marco looked steadfastly at the floor.

"Ah, Señor Alonso," he said. "Here is the paper you asked for. And the pens. And the ink." Marco kept his eyes on the floor as the fat scribe handed the things one by one to Alonso. Alonso handed them to Marco, who took them without looking up. The scribe did not look carefully at the boy. The men spoke and laughed as they traded money for paper. Finally, Marco and Alonzo turned to leave the shop. Marco's heart began to race the race of a person about to escape. The door was only three feet away now. Two feet.

"Good-bye, Señor Alonso! Good-bye, young man!" The scribe's voice rang merrily behind them.

"Good-bye, Señor," said Alonso. Marco said nothing.

"Marco, turn and say good-bye to the gentleman," urged Alonso.

Marco stopped, but did not turn around. Alonso put a hand on his shoulder and turned him. Marco's eyes met the scribe's. The scribe's mouth hung open. Then, at the same time, both of them glanced at the ceiling. A wide hole in the straw roof had been covered from the outside with a canvas. Marco and the scribe lowered their gazes to look on each other. The scribe's mouth hung open. Then, as Marco watched, the man began to laugh. The laugh shook his whole, large body. Red faced, he laughed even louder. Alonso laughed too.

"Well then, we will leave you to your private joke," said Alonso. "Come, Marco." The two walked out of the scribe's building. The scribe's laughter rang down the street until long after they had made their way back to the inn.

Alonso chuckled. "He laughs well, no? I wonder what he laughed at."

Marco shrugged.

———

Marco slept that night in a bed. It was the first time since he had left Spain. In the morning (a morning on which Alonso had to shake him and shake him before he awoke), they went to the docks. Alonso carried his sea bag.

Marco carried Alonso's paper, pens, and ink.

"What is my job?" asked Marco, walking fast to keep up.

"Eh?" asked Alonso.

"My job. You said yesterday that you had a special job for me."

Alonso shrugged. "Oh, it isn't much. I have met many of the men who are preparing for this voyage. One of them has become lonely. He lost his son to the sea. He seems a good enough man. If you will take it, you have the job of comforting him. You lost your father to the sea, no?"

Marco nodded.

"Then you may know how this man feels."

Marco shrugged. Comforting him? He would try to do what Alonso asked, but the task of comforting someone after the loss of a dear one seemed a heavy one. Marco's pace slowed.

Alonso turned to face him. "You can do this job, yes?"

Marco shrugged. "Yes," he said, thinly.

"Then come. These are the ships now."

At the crowded docks, two ships were loading. Men swarmed up and down the gangplanks carrying boxes and sacks of flour. People pushed past each other on deck. There had been fifteen men on *La Juana*, and *La Juana* had been a much bigger ship than either of these. On these two smallish ships, what must have been a hundred people marched about, preparing to sail. Marco had never seen so much activity.

"Ai, Alonso!" called a voice from the rail. Marco looked up. Garrido stood in the bow. "You are late!" He shouted with a grin.

"Yes," shouted Alonso back. "But look what I have with me! A street rat to help me push barrels and crates about!"

Garrido laughed. "Ai, Marco! You found him, then!" Garrido moved quickly to the gangplank and met Alonso and Marco at the bottom. He lifted Marco into a powerful hug, and then plopped him back onto the dock, smiling.

"Alonso, he disappears for three days to find you, once he realizes—"

"—Once he realizes that he can never keep track of all his work by himself," interrupted Alonso.

Garrido raised his eyebrows. "Ah, you have not told—"

Alonso stood on Garrido's foot, and Garrido fell silent. "Come, boy. We go aboard."

The three friends climbed the gangplank. In a moment, thought Marco, I will be on another journey, with food to eat and friends around. A world with no hunger or enemies. That is truly a New World!

At the top of the gangplank, Marco paused to wait for a man who was bent over, wrestling a keg up onto his shoulder. With a heave, the man stood straight, facing

Marco. Marco yelped—his breath frozen in his chest. The keg tumbled from the man's shoulder, popping its cork as it hit the deck. With a hiss, dry beans spilled around the man's feet.

"S-Señor Matanza ... I ... " stammered Marco.

"You!" gasped Matanza. He took a step toward Marco.

"Hold, Matanza," said Alonso gruffly. He clapped a hand on Marco's shoulder. "The business between you is finished. The boy is remorseful, and has come here to work."

"But—," from Matanza.

"—He is also under my protection," said Alonso.

Marco could not understand what he heard. His business with Matanza, finished? What did Alonso mean? Marco's gaze fell to Matanza's belt. There, from a thick strap hung a familiar pouch. But how—

"Keep your eyes to yourself, rat," snarled Matanza. His hand went to the pouch, covering it.

" No ... you misunderstand ... I did not look to—"

"—Pedrito!" shouted Matanza. Across the deck, a boy came scampering. "Scoop these beans back into the barrel."

Matanza's mouth opened as though he would say something else. But he closed it again, and stormed off toward the hold.

The boy that Matanza had called stooped and began to

work. He wore a handsome shirt and trousers, and his feet were bare. He worked quickly, first tipping the barrel upright and then scooping the beans with his cupped hands. As the boy worked, bent over the barrel, Marco could see only the top of his head. The boy had dark hair, cropped ragged and short. The boy glanced up at Marco.

The glance was enough. Marco's eyes went wide.

Juanita.

She spoke, "Much better for two boys" (she said the word "boys" very loudly) "to be aboard a ship bound for new lands than to be hungry in the streets of San Juan, no?" She smiled sheepishly. "It is lucky that there are no girls about," (she said the word "girls" very loudly). "Who knows what might happen to a girl among a rowdy crew like this?"

Marco gaped. Silence.

"My name is Pedrito," said Juanita (she said the word "Pedrito" very loudly). "It is nice to meet you."

"It ... it is nice to meet you, too," said Marco. He didn't know what else to say.

Alonso began to push Marco forward, guiding him through the activity on deck. He held to Marco's shoulder, and with a gentle push or pull kept Marco out of the way of swinging crates and jostling feet. Garrido followed them.

As they passed the hold, Marco heard strange noises—

the chatter of men working, but also deep groaning, like a huge man crying out in pain. He shrugged Alonso's hand away, and went to the edge of the hold. He peered down into the dim light. Below him, men shuffled back and forth, stacking boxes and barrels, then one of them pulled something startling into the light.

Marco blinked. "Is that a cow?" He looked again, "Two cows?"

Garrido chuckled. "It is good to have a genius aboard ship. We all thought they were alligators." Marco laughed.

"Later, I will show you what is down in the hold," said Alonso. "Cows, and more. Horses. Some chickens. Four pigs. Because you are a boy, you will enjoy seeing them today. Tomorrow, you will enjoy it less. A week from now, you will be holding your nose and wishing they had stayed in San Juan. But you will be glad of milk and eggs and pork in *La Florida*."

Marco watched the cows for a moment more, and then followed Alonso toward the aft lines. They stopped beneath the starboard shrouds. Alonso turned to Garrido. "Up there?" he asked.

Garrido nodded, grinning.

Alonso turned to Marco. "Is it a good day for you, to be here?" he asked.

"A day of surprises," said Marco. The truth was, he had

been aboard for less than five minutes, and already he was weary from the excitement.

"Surprises? What, that Matanza is here? He is a sailor, yes? Where else would a sailor be than on the most important voyage ever to leave San Juan? Surprised that his gold came back to him, in the hands of the same boy that took it from you? Bah. A boy, because he has no use for money, stumbles across Matanza's pouch and sees an opportunity. He takes it. Surprise? Bah."

"Perhaps more of a surprise than you know," muttered Marco, under his breath.

Alonso continued. "A surprise that your friend Alonso found you? Don't be surprised. We worked on the ship many days before she is ready to go, no? I was here. Matanza was here. As soon as I learned how Matanza's pouch came back to him, I began to look. Three days I searched. It is no surprise that much hard work pays off in the end. So you see, this is not a day of surprises. Compare this day to the day it yet will be, and it is a regular day. A boring day."

"What do you mean?" asked Marco.

Alonso raised his eyebrows and smiled. "You speak of a day filled with surprises? How do you like this?" He craned his neck, put his hand to his mouth, and called up into the rigging. Garrido looked up too. He was still grinning.

"Eh, Jimenez! Come down to the deck please?" Alonso's call rang out.

A shouted response from above.

Alonso turned to Marco. "This is the man I told you about. It will be easy, I think, for you to become friends."

Marco stared up into the rigging, squinting into the sun. A shape descended. Marco looked up at the man's boots—his legs worked step by step down the ladder. Then the man stood on deck. He looked at Alonso.

"You need me to help you with something?"

"I need you to help me with this boy," said Alonso. And then, to Marco, "Marco, this is Señor Jimenez."

Marco looked at the man. "*Buenos dias*, Señor Jimenez. It is funny. Jimenez is my—"

"Marco!" The man, wild-eyed, took Marco by the shoulders.

For a silent moment, Marco looked at the man. He was muscular and lean from a long time at sea. His long hair was pulled back, and a thick, dark beard covered his face. His eyes were clear and green. Like Marco's own.

"Papà?" whispered the boy.

With a long shout, the man sank to his knees and folded Marco into his arms.

"Papà!" Marco clutched wildly at his father's neck. His throat coughed up great sobs.

"Marco!" shouted Jimenez into the sky. "It's Marco! My son! My son!"

Marco's father shouted, and Marco sobbed. Other crew stopped what they were doing, and turned to notice them. Over several seconds, work on the ship came to a halt.

Over and over, Garrido slapped Alonso on the back. Great, happy tears rolled down his cheeks. Through it all, Alonso spoke.

"I did a good job with this surprise, no?" he said. "I found Marco, but I held my tongue so I can see the surprise on his face. And there it is, yes?"

Marco and his father never heard Alonso.

The sobs came and came. Marco's father rocked him back and forth. The man that Marco had pretended to be melted away now, further and further away with each sob. As the moments passed, Marco became each minute more a boy—a boy of ten, in his father's arms.

After many long moments, Marco heard boot heels on the deck—approaching them. He and his father both lifted their heads to see a man standing before them.

Marco recognized the man. It was Juan Ponce de Leon.

Marco's father stood, holding Marco's hand. Father and son wiped tears from their cheeks.

"Jimenez, yes?" asked Juan Ponce.

"Yes sir. Pedro Jimenez. At your service, sir," said

Marco's father.

"And this is your son?"

"*Sì Señor*. My son Marco. He has been lost to me for more than two years. I received word that my family had died in Spain. But it seems now that they did not all die," Marco's father squeezed Marco's hand.

"So it seems. My congratulations to you both," said Juan Ponce. He looked at Marco.

"And you. Marco, is it?"

"*Sì, Señor*. Marco, sir," said Marco

"Marco, like Marco Polo," said Juan Ponce. "Do you know who that was?"

"I am sorry, I do not, sir."

"Marco Polo traveled with his father and uncle to China, over the silk road. Seventeen years he was there. He wrote a book about his adventures. Columbus carried this book. Did you know that I knew Columbus?"

"I did, sir. You came to the New World with him."

Juan Ponce smiled. "Yes, I came to the New World with Columbus. And now it is time to push still further on. You are a member of my crew, yes?"

"Yes sir, I came aboard with Señor Jerèz, sir."

Juan Ponce looked at Alonso. "You are Señor Jerèz?"

"Yes sir," said Alonso. Garrido wiped his eyes on his shirtsleeve.

"You are my cargo man for this ship, yes?"

"I am, sir," said Alonso.

"Very good," said Juan Ponce. "I also put you in charge of reuniting all small boys of the crew with any of their long-lost fathers, also of the crew."

"Done, sir," said Alonso with a wide smile. The men of the crew laughed. Juan Ponce turned to face them. Then he glanced back at Marco.

"To have a Marco on the voyage is a good omen," he whispered. Then he addressed the crew.

"Since I have your attention ... is the crew all here? Yes, come up from the gangplank ... and from the hold, listen up here. You, on the ratlines! Hold for a moment, eh?"

The crew fell silent. Juan Ponce began.

"My cabin is on *La Fuente*, the other ship, and I am glad to speak for a moment with you, the crew and passengers of the *Leonor*. San Juan Bautista has been my home for more than a dozen years—and Hispaniola before that. I look to the east, and the ocean is like a road deep with wagon ruts. Many have traveled that road. Some of you have traveled it many times. Travelers sleep through that voyage when the weather stays fair. But now we look to the west, and there will be no sleeping. We are sinking the prows of these two ships like plowshares in a new field. To the west, few journeys have been taken. Eight years ago I went there with my crew, and we found *La Florida*. We found the great current that carries ships from the New World back to the old. We found much. I was a younger man eight years ago. Eight years ago, all the eyes that watched the New World watched us. But we did not stay, and now the world watches Cortes. It watches him with admiration and with fear.

Now we, with two small ships—with a few men and a hold full of bleating animals—we go to the new land. We go to discover what we can and to build what we can. It is the journey of Juan Ponce de Leon. But I am one man only, between two ships loaded to the gunwales with men, and the New World waits. As for me, I go to plant crops, and to read King Charles' Requirement to the natives—loathe as I am to read it."

"What's a 'Requirement,'" asked Marco.

Alonso leaned toward Marco, "Let Juan Ponce speak. There will be talk of the Requirement later."

Juan Ponce continued. "Can we turn the eyes of the world away from Cortes? From Cortes, the world learns that if you polish your armor and wander into the jungle with an army—if you kill enough Indians—you can win the respect of anyone you can hold at sword point." Juan Ponce paused, then spoke again. "What will the world learn from us?" he said.

Juan Ponce raised his voice. "Build a town in the wilderness," he continued, "surrounded by green fields—build a colony that brings forth the bounty of the New World. In a New World, where the crown has spilled gold and blood alike trying to beat back the natives, build a colony where the natives—pacified, and subject to the crown—walk among us without weapons and without fear. Build that colony, and once you've built it, live there! Live there, rather than planting a stick in the ground and scuttling back to Spain like Columbus. Do that, and the world will stare."

The crew was silent. Juan Ponce turned a full circle to see them all. Then he spoke again.

"Now, gentlemen. We go to *La Florida*."

A cheer erupted from the deck of the ship. Hats were waved, and Marco's father lifted him up and hugged him close. The cheer was caught up and echoed by the second ship. Juan Ponce laughed, and turned to Marco.

"Do you think the men on the other ship even know why they cheer, Marco Polo?"

Marco grinned and shrugged.

"It was a good rehearsal for what will be a better speech when I give it on the other ship. Maybe before we get to *La Florida* I will get that chance, no?"

Marco laughed. So did his father. Juan Ponce

continued.

"It is a good day for you, Jimenez. Later, you take a good long time with your son. Now, though, let's get to sea, eh?"

"Sì Señor," said Marco's father.

It might have been nice to end Juan Ponce's speech with a glorious unfurling of the sails, and a swift push off from the docks as the men cheered. As it was, there was an hour's work more to do. The hold was soundly loaded and catalogued, Alonso checking crates and sacks and making marks with his pen. The crew's luggage was stowed below decks. Duty rosters were announced and posted. Men introduced themselves to each other, shaking hands as they came together in one task or another. Marco watched his father lift one end of a great sack, with Matanza on the other end. Juan Ponce left the *Leonor*, and boarded *La Fuente*.

Marco himself loaded chickens above decks and then helped Alonso below. He forgot his questions about the Requirement—whatever it was. Finally, and without fanfare, the foresails went up. First one ship, then another, slowly pulled away from the docks.

The energy of Juan Ponce's speech had mellowed. Men rubbed sore muscles and nursed blisters. Behind them in San Juan, people walked the docks as usual. No cheering crowd had gathered there. No cannons fired in salute.

As yet, it seemed, they had not turned any heads.

Marco stood at the rail with Alonso. The men had grown quieter. The frenzy of preparing for the journey had ceased, and the ship moved into its sailing rhythm. The other ship plowed slowly beside them.

Alonso turned away from the sea, and looked over the ship. Across the deck, Matanza loaded Juanita up with a large barrel, and pointed in the direction of the firebox. Near the forecastle, Garrido whistled as he yanked on the halyard. Marco's father worked in the shrouds above, checking lines. Soon, he would come down again to the deck, and to Marco.

"See, Marco," said Alonso. "Treasure hunters, villains, visionaries, miracles, and old men wishing to be young. It is like the whole New World, all aboard one tiny ship, no?"

Chapter 9

If Marco had ever suspected that being aboard the *Leonor* would be anything like his trip aboard *La Juana*, he was mistaken. Coming to San Juan aboard *La Juana*, he had been a bedridden guest. The sailors had been kind to him—tousled his hair when he wandered onto deck, and brought him the best bits of food from the firebox.

Now, he was crew like the rest. His food was just like

everyone else's—pickled herring for breakfast, stew with peas
and garlic at dinner, and cold stew and a hunk of cheese
for supper. Marco worked all day—mostly in the hold,
feeding the animals and cleaning up after them. The first
day, it had been wonderful. Marco had never been so close
to so many animals at once. He stroked the big, firm necks
of the horses, and reached beneath fat chickens for warm
eggs. He ran his hands through the thick wool of the sheep,
and wrinkled his nose at the pigs. The pleasures of being in
the hold with the animals lasted one day only. The next
day, he shoveled dung until his hands blistered. Day after
day it was like that—Marco lowered a bucket on a rope into
the hold. Then he climbed down the steps, grabbed the
shovel, filled the bucket, climbed back up, pulled up the
bucket after him, and emptied it over the side. Then back
down into the hold with the bucket, and with Marco. Over
and over he did this. He hated the animals.

Juanita sometimes worked alongside Marco. He
remembered to call her Pedrito whenever he spoke to her,
but he didn't have to remember often. Their time together
was filled with awkward silence. It was even more awkward
when Matanza would come and stand above the hatch,
calling to Pedrito for one thing or another. Marco in the
hold, Juanita beside him, and Matanza above—those were
the most difficult moments.

But the journey wasn't all old enemies and animal dung. Marco was always anxious to work with his father, and such chances came often.

"Come up here, Marco, eh?" Marco's father shouted down into the darkness of the hold one afternoon. Marco leaned his shovel against the hull, whacked the feed dust from his hands, and climbed to the deck. His father stood with a coil of rope and a smooth piece of wood in his hands.

"Help me mark speed?" asked his father.

Marco grinned. "Yes! How do you do it?"

"Come. I will show you." Marco's father took Marco to the gunwale. He leaned out, and motioned for Marco to do the same.

"See that long rib of wood—the one that runs up-and-down-ways, starting just below the rail here and ending just above the waterline down there?"

"I see it," said Marco.

"That's a futtock rider. There's one every few feet."

"Yes," said Marco. "I can see them. Every few feet from the front of the ship to the back."

"From bow to stern, yes." Marco's father pointed forward, toward the bow. "I will go as far forward as the first futtock rider." He pointed backward, to the stern. "You run now," he said. "Climb the ladder to the quarterdeck, and then all the way back to the poop deck."

"Poop deck?"

"Yes, Marco, the highest deck, beyond the quarterdeck, above the big cabin. Climb to that deck and stand above the last rider."

Marco nodded.

"I'll drop this log in the water." Marco's father held up the smooth piece of wood. There was a hole in one end of it. The thin rope was tied through the hole. "When I drop the log, you begin to count. When the log reaches the water right below you, stop counting and raise your arm. Use the futtock rider as a marker to help you see when the log passes. Remember the number you counted, and tell it to me."

Marco nodded again. He padded across the main deck, scurried up the ladder to the quarterdeck, and then again up the ladder to the poop. To the edge of the bulwark he went, looking for the futtock rider. He found it.

"I am ready, Papà!"

"Here I go, then!" Marco's father dropped the wood piece in the water with a hollow splash. The log floated toward Marco's end of the ship. In the bow, his father quickly paid out the rope.

Marco counted. One, two, three, four, five, almost here, and now. Marco shot his hand into the air.

Marco's father tugged the rope back, reeling the log back in.

"Good, Marco," he said. "How many?"

"Seven," said Marco, climbing down the ladders. He scampered to where his father stood.

"You are patient with your numbers, Marco." Marco's father shrugged, "This is good. I counted nine."

"So how fast are we going?" asked Marco.

"Well, it looks like we're moving one boat-length every count of nine," said Marco's father. "And if we know how long our ship is, then we can figure out in our heads how long it will take to travel two boat-lengths, or a hundred." As he spoke, the log came over the rail and rattled on the deck. "It works sometimes," Marco's father said. "Someday there will be a better way to mark speed."

Marco bent and began to gather up the wet rope into coils. After a moment, he looked up. His father stood still, looking at Marco. To Marco, he seemed sad.

"Papà?" Marco asked.

"It is good to see you," said Marco's father.

"It is good to see you, too," said Marco.

Marco's father looked at the deck. Then he spoke again. "To have missed two years. It is difficult. I do not like to think about that."

Marco listened.

"I should not have gone to sea," continued Marco's father. "I should have stayed with you."

Marco listened.

"Someone wrote a letter to me. A letter that said that my family had died. I never saw the letter. Another man saw it, and then the letter was lost, and he told me. Without you and Mamà, there was no reason to go home. I stayed in San Juan."

"I remember the letter," said Marco. "A priest in Càdiz wrote it. After Mamà died, they did not know what to do with me. I did not want to live with the priests. I wanted to live with you. I watched for your boat every day."

"I thought you were dead, Marco."

"I thought you were dead, too, Papà."

"It is a great gift to me that you are still alive, my son. And a miracle that you are here. And to be brought to me by pirates!"

"I like that you are here too, Papà."

There was a short silence between them. Then Marco's father spoke.

"Tell me what is between you and that other man, Matanza, and the boy who is with him."

Marco rolled his eyes, and took a deep breath. He told his father of the storm aboard *La Juana*, and the pouch of gold coins. He talked of meeting Juanita (though in his story he spoke of her as a boy named Pedrito), and of going to Juan Ponce's house for food. Marco's father laughed.

"I lived in San Juan for two years and I never so much as saw Juan Ponce de Leon. But you wash up from the sea, and go to eat supper at his house!"

Marco told his father how the gold had gone missing again, and about how it now hung on Matanza's belt.

"Suddenly I see," said Marco's father.

"See what?"

"A few of us were aboard before the journey, preparing the ship. Matanza was among us. One day, a boy came aboard and told Matanza he had something to give him—something hidden away. Somehow, the boy knew Matanza's name and had found him. Matanza left for an hour. He came back with a pouch of gold on his belt, and the boy has been with him ever since." Marco's father chuckled. "The boy must have known that carrying a bag of gold in San Juan might have been dangerous."

"So I have heard, myself," muttered Marco under his breath.

His father continued. "For a crafty child like that— what's his name—Pedrito?"

"Something like that," muttered Marco.

"Pedrito, then. In any case, a pouch full of gold coins could buy either a lifetime of cassava roots, or—if a child were cunning enough—passage on a ship to the New World. For a child like Pedrito—one with brains in his head and a taste for adventure, but no home to speak of—it must have been an easy choice. He must have made a deal with Matanza for passage on this voyage."

Marco remained sullen. "It's a wonder that Matanza didn't just take the gold and leave Pedrito alone—or dead."

Macro's father shrugged. "Matanza surely thinks he came out ahead." He held up a finger. "He's got a pouch of gold swinging from his belt—" he held up another finger, "—and a cabin boy to command as he will. I've watched them, though. It seems to me that it is the boy—and not Matanza—that has the other one wrapped around his little finger. Pedrito has salvaged his future—gone from living in the alleys of San Juan to riding the same breeze that brings glory to Juan Ponce. For the boy, it was a good trade. Poor Matanza."

Marco laughed. His father interrupted him.

"Before you laugh, Marco, think of what Matanza's little bag of gold has done. Matanza's losing of it made enemies of you and he. Your losing of it made enemies of you and the boy. For Matanza, getting it back meant saddling himself with a child that he does not love—a child that will burden him in the New World and beyond. The gold has passed through the hands of each of you, and each of you thought honor a small price to pay for such a thing. And now, here you are, all together—left to look at each other over a boatload of your shared sins."

Marco spoke. "I had been taken by pirates. I stole the pouch to choose my own fate. I though I was choosing the way of a man."

"A man, if he admired Matanza's pouch, would have congratulated him and then gone out and made his own. It is so that men do," said Marco's father.

"But what about men like Matanza?" asked Marco without thinking. He regretted the question as soon as he asked it.

"Is this what you wish to be? Like Matanza? There are many like Matanza. They are grown, but none of them are men."

Marco fell silent. He looked at the deck.

"Thank you for teaching me to mark speed, Papà." Marco said it quietly, and then turned for the hold again. His father's voice stopped him.

"It is difficult to be a father again," he said.

Marco didn't know how to answer this, and so he didn't.

There was a strained silence between Marco and his father for the rest of the day. When night fell, the tired crew went to the forecastle to talk and to sleep. Marco had his own hammock—a great sheet of canvas slung from the beams below the forecastle deck—though the first few nights of the voyage he had spent sharing his father's hammock, his arm across his father's chest, and his head resting on his father's shoulder. Tonight, though, Marco went to his own hammock. One by one, the men of the crew filled the forecastle. Only a few stayed behind, checking yards or preparing for watch. The sea was still. The bleating of the animals in the hold gathered itself into the deep, quiet breath of sleep. The shouting that underscored the daytime chores dwindled into soft talk and laughter.

Marco listened.

"Hang," said one old sailor. "This trip's got my nerves in a knot."

"What? You afraid of ghosts in the New World?" someone joked. Some laughed.

"Ghosts, nar!" said the first sailor. "It's these passengers. I go to sea with sailors, same as you, right? But down in that hold we got priests, carpenters, soldiers—"

"—cows, chickens, pigs!" said another voice. More laughter.

"The animals I can take," said the first sailor. "But it doesn't do me good to see a soldier sleeping in the hold while I'm smearing pitch on the seams. Heavens, I say the animals on a ship can do as they please, but the humans ought to share the work, right?"

Another voice spoke up. "You want to berth in the smelly hold with the animals? You want to stay down there in the dark, and eat the poor rations? I'm sure any of those yawning soldiers would change you places!"

"Indeed. You've ferried rum and silks, haven't you?" said another voice. It was Alonso. "This is the same, only the cargo is colonists. Your work hasn't changed—only your mood." There was laughter at this.

"My mood?" said the first sailor. "They've got hands, don't they, those down below? Let them—"

"Let them do what they came to do," said Alonso. "Let you and I do the ship things, and the priests do the priest things, and the soldiers do the soldier things."

"Hang," said the first sailor, and then he was silent. Then, "All I know is, after the work we do on this ship, when we get to the New World and some savage comes at me swinging a club around his head, I'm going to stand with my arms folded. It'll be my turn to rest then. And one of those soldiers had better come running, and he'd better do some soldiering!" The crew laughed.

"Laugh, then!" said the sailor. "You think I'm tired and angry now. Just wait until I've a great gashing hole in my head from some savage club, after all I did to keep those idiots from falling into the sea!" The crew roared.

"Hang, all of you!" said the first sailor. Then he was silent.

"I say I will work enough for ten men in trade for the prize that waits for us in *La Florida*." This was Matanza now.

"We would be happy if you would do the work of one man!" someone shouted.

"Come here and say that, you—"

"—I agree with Matanza," interrupted a voice. It was Alonso. Marco was surprised. Alonso continued. "To find the Fountain would be worth all the work, yes?" he said, calmly.

"I do not speak of the Fountain," said Matanza.

"Oh?" said Alonso. "Then I change my mind. I do not agree with Matanza." Marco smiled.

"You think this journey is about a fountain of magic water?" said Matanza. "You believe that tale?"

"A tale, maybe," said Alonso. "But a tale told by old men and young men for more years than there are coins in your silly purse—and told to Juan Ponce by men who told it not as a false tale, but as a true one."

Matanza countered. "Listen, old man. Preparing for this journey—or even in his great speech to us on the day we departed—did you hear Juan Ponce mention the Fountain even one time?"

"It is silly, Matanza," said Alonso. "Everyone knows that Juan Ponce goes to search for the fountain that will make men young—"

"But did you hear him say it?" Matanza spoke the words slowly.

"He did not say it because everyone knows it," said Alonso. The cheer had gone from his voice.

Matanza spoke again. "Listen, all of you. This voyage is about glory in the New World. There will be gold for the crown, and for us. There will be slaves to sell and to keep. Juan Ponce is a man of business. And his business—if any of you have paid any attention—is subduing the people of the New World, under the heel of Spain."

"Go to sleep!" yelled someone.

"Go to sleep yourself!" said Matanza. He turned to the first sailor who had spoken. "You, with the great gashing hole in your head. You're tired of work? *La Florida* is covered with rich land, and natives to work it. If you are here for something else, you are a fool."

Another voice spoke. It was Garrido. "Your talk is too big for my head, Matanza," he said. "I am here for the money promised me as a member of the crew. We build this colony, and then I go home and find another trip to go on, just like I have done all my life."

"See? A fool," said Matanza. The crew laughed.

Talk in the forecastle ebbed, until no more than a few whispered conversations accompanied the lapping of the water against the hull. One by one, lanterns were put out, and the conversation died altogether. Marco lay awake in the dark with his thoughts. He had heard Juan Ponce talk of the journey—heard all his friends at the wedding make fun of the search for the fountain of magic water. Yet he had also heard what those same friends called Juan Ponce: the Scourge of the Caribs.

But that was what his friends said about him, not what Juan Ponce said about himself. If Marco remembered, Juan Ponce had remained silent as his friends spoke of such things. So where was the heart of Juan Ponce de Leon? Marco could not sleep, thinking.

His eyes were closed, but Marco was still awake when his father padded in from watch. His father came to where Marco's hammock hung, and placed a hand for a moment on Marco's forehead. The hand was rough and cool.

"Sleep on, son," he whispered. "If Juan Ponce is right, tomorrow we land."

Marco did not move. Marco's father climbed into his own hammock, across from Marco's. In a few moments, Marco heard his father's breath change, and he knew he had fallen asleep.

Still, Marco lay awake. For two years, he had longed to find his father. Now, his father was here. He was here, and he thought Marco a thief. *My father*, thought Marco, *must see me in the same way that I see Matanza*. The thought was unbearable; unbearable, but true. Marco the thief cried himself softly to sleep.

———

That night, Marco dreamed that the ship reached shore. Men from the crew lowered the sails, and worked the windlass to drop anchor. In the dream, Marco, Juan Ponce, Alonso, Garrido, and Marco's father boarded a smaller boat and rowed toward shore. When they arrived, Marco's father climbed from the bow and began to pull the boat up onto the sand. Marco leaped from the stern to help. But in Marco's dream, the sea was deeper than he thought. He went underwater, and came up sputtering. He flailed his arms, trying to lay a hand on the wale of the boat. But a current dragged him away, and out to sea. Marco's father turned to see him. He raised his hand in a fist, and shouted out to Marco. "Stupid boy!" he said. "What have you done!" The men on ship watched Marco, but none threw him a line. "When you get to Spain, swim for land!" one sailor shouted. "Swim for land! Land!"

"Land!" Marco awoke from the dream with a start. Men

streamed from the forecastle, hastily pulling on shirts or pants.

"Land!" came the cry again. Marco tumbled from his hammock. A strong hand helped him to his feet. It was his father. Pedro Jimenez grinned at his son. Marco smiled wanly back. The angry image of Marco's father was still fresh in his mind from his dream.

Marco rushed from the forecastle and up the ladder to the forecastle deck. Crewmen gathered at the rail. Priests, soldiers, carpenters and farmers swarmed up from the hold as well. Marco could hear the cries of the animals below. Sails swung overhead.

On the horizon was a ribbon of dark land. It stretched in either direction, as far as Marco could see. If this was an island, it was an enormous one.

"At irons!" cried a voice.

"At irons?" asked Marco.

"It's when the sails are parallel with the wind, and can't catch it. It's how we stay in one place, even with the sails up," answered his father.

"At irons!" repeated another voice. The ship was still.

"What's going on? Why don't we go to shore?" asked Marco.

"We wait for orders from *La Fuente*," said Marco's father. "Juan Ponce will choose the place where we land."

La Fuente stood at irons as well, off the port bow. Her crew gathered at the rail, just like the crew of the Leonor. From where he stood, Marco could see Juan Ponce. The explorer stood on the forecastle deck, gesturing and talking with La Fuente's captain. Marco could not hear what they said.

"What's he waiting for?" Marco heard someone say.

The crew fell into silence, waiting for orders. Then, finally, they heard a shout from the other ship. La Fuente's foresail swiveled to catch the wind, and the ship turned. Moments later, the Leonor matched her.

But Juan Ponce was not headed for shore. He ran his ship parallel to the land, picking up speed.

"Where are we going?" asked Marco.

His father shrugged. "Maybe Juan Ponce doesn't like the look of the place."

"But this is the place, isn't it? La Florida?"

"Patience, boy," said a voice. It was Alonso. He put his hand on the top of Marco's head. "Eight years ago, Juan Ponce sailed to shore in La Florida with a big smile, and Calusa Indians threw spears at him from the trees. He will choose a landing place with great care, I think."

"What kind of place is he looking for?" asked Marco.

Alonso pointed at the dark trees on the shore. "Juan Ponce looks for a landing with wide open sand and a long way between trees."

"Is that all?"

"'Is that all'? What do you mean, 'is that all'? Is it not enough? Look at those wooded areas." Alonso pointed toward shore. "Behind each of those trees an enemy could be hiding."

Marco's eyebrows went up.

"Besides," continued Alonso, "if there are no trees where we build our settlement then there are no trees that we will have to pull out of the ground to make room for it."

Marco nodded.

Cautiously, *La Fuente* worked her way along the coast.

Breathless, the crew and passengers of the *Leonor* followed and watched.

But the breathlessness wore off, and Alonso spoke again. "It is good if the place has water nearby as well," he said.

Marco looked at his friend. "The Fountain? This is what Juan Ponce looks for?"

Alonso chuckled. "Even better!" he said. "But I am afraid that for now Juan Ponce thinks mostly of using the water for thirsty horses and tender crops."

Again and again, for hours at a time, *La Fuente* slowed, turned inland, hesitated, and pulled away. The Leonor stayed safely back, following *La Fuente* each time the ship headed further upland. In the end, the crew lost interest.

They turned from the deck and began to attend to their duties. Passengers, too, began to move distractedly away from the rail. Some stayed on deck. Others went below. This went on all day: stop the ship, wait for *La Fuente* to sniff the air, and then continue on. By nightfall, they had traveled far—still in sight of land, but no closer to it.

In the morning, the dance began again. Put the ship at irons, slow to a stop, wait for *La Fuente*, then move again.

Marco was below, tossing a slop of old biscuits and stew to the pigs, when he heard a shout. He dropped his bucket and climbed the steps to the deck. *La Fuente* was ahead of them, plowing for shore. The *Leonor* erupted in a frenzy of chattering sailors, and a dance of shifting sails and lines.

"We're landing?" Marco found Alonso.

Marco moved to the rail, and leaned over the side of the ship. He could see the white sea-bottom moving under them. Along the glistening sand, dark shapes raced.

"Mermaids!" shouted Marco. He pointed down at them.

Garrido was passing by. "Dolphins," he corrected. "The New World is wondrous—but perhaps not so wondrous as to be guarded by mer-people, eh?" he grinned at Marco.

The dolphins sped through the water, and then broke the surface, their grey backs rising above the waves, and then disappearing again. To Marco, they may as well have been mermaids.

Chapter 10

"You can't stay angry with me forever," she had said. The words had come while they were still days and days from land. When he heard the words, Marco had turned his back on Juanita. He'd prove her wrong. He'd stay angry. Forever.

It might have worked if they had been on separate ships. As it was, at sea their paths had crossed many times every day. Marco's anger at Juanita, try as he might, had begun to soften. Had someone asked, Marco would not have called Juanita a friend. But even after the ships landed, when there was enough space to be as far apart as they wished, they found themselves together often. They were, after all, the only children on the voyage.

But it wasn't just the relationship between Marco and Juanita (who, remarkably, was still Pedrito to the rest of the colony) that had changed. Life in the New World had come as a blow to everyone on the voyage. There was a moment on the first day, as the ships lay at anchor, when the crew and colonists had wiggled their toes in the sand and heard the breeze in the tall palms. It was a moment that filled each man on the voyage with gladness and confidence in himself—as if the world had conspired with each man to breathe success into whatever private venture he planned in his heart.

But planting crops, building shelters, and finding water were more difficult than anyone had anticipated. And with land to be cleared of stout palmettos before it could be built upon (or even traveled easily), the work ate up all the space in a man's heart that once could be spared for grudges. There was far too much work—and it was far too difficult—for any man to do alone. Behind plows, sewing canvases, and beneath water buckets, Marco worked beside

Matanza, Juanita, and even—on some occasions—Juan Ponce himself. Had there been a moment to gather his thoughts, Marco might have numbered certain of those that surrounded him as enemies—certain others as friends. But there was no moment. Work flowed into work, and then into sleep, and then into work again.

Water in buckets came around to everyone at intervals throughout each day. Marco was always glad when it came. Alonso always held each ladleful of water carefully before he drank it. He would sometimes dip a finger into the water before he drank it, and suck the water from his finger thoughtfully.

"You still look old," Marco would say. "This water must be nothing but water." Then he would laugh.

Alonso would laugh too, but not as loudly.

Marco watched Juan Ponce sometimes as the explorer drank from the bucket. He hoped to see a change come over the man's face—the look of discovery. But if Juan Ponce was thinking of the magical fountain as he drank, he didn't show it. He mopped his brow with his sleeve, threw back the ladle, and let the water dribble over his beard. Then he chunked the ladle back in the bucket. If there was a fountain of magical water on the island, no one (except Alonso) seemed to be looking very hard for it.

Now, Marco and Juanita were making bricks. They

filled adobe frames with a mixture of mud, sand, and straw. The frames lay in a line before Marco. Marco packed the stiff mixture firmly into a frame, sweat drying on his forehead. Then he moved to the next empty frame. Behind him, Juanita quickly lifted the frame from around the wet brick. Then she scurried around in front of Marco and laid her frame on the ground at the end of the line. The bricks dried slowly in the sun. They stretched out behind the two children in long columns. Juanita was speaking.

"...and the priest said that he won't feel comfortable in the New World until there's a real church, not an adobe hut like he's got now. But I told him ... "

Marco wasn't listening. He was counting.

"...245, 246, 247 ... " he counted. "Looks like we'll get three hundred by suppertime."

"Really?" Juanita interrupted her own story. "That's thirty more than yesterday. And nearly seventy more than we were doing six weeks ago."

"You say 'we,'" said Marco, "as if you had helped any."

"Helped any!" Juanita bristled. "I have hauled adobe frames without rest for weeks! And before that, I fed the animals that plowed those fields!" She pointed just beyond the wooden stable, where a team of horses flicked flies from their haunches.

"Yes," said Marco. "Sixteen weeks in the New World.

Sixteen weeks of your mouth working twice as hard as the rest of you."

Juanita's mouth hung open. "You sit there playing in the mud and you tell me that I'm lazy?"

Marco laughed. He was joking about Juanita being lazy. No one had been lazy. But teasing Juanita had worked her into a frenzy—and Marco enjoyed it. He enjoyed it too much to stop now.

"It's alright to admit it, Pedrito," he said. "Even lazy people can learn to be productive. It's like this." He held out his right hand. It was covered in mud and straw. His palm faced up. "You do the work," he said. Then he held out his left hand, palm up. "And you ... " Marco's voice trailed off. In his imagination, he saw Pollito's small, white hands, placed just like Marco's were now. In Juanita's place, he imagined himself. So long, it seemed, since Pollito had taken his lazy friend, Marco, aside on the wharf at Càdiz. So long since Marco had stormed off to be hit on the head by pirates. In his imagination, Marco looked at Pollito's hands—one empty hand, for the milk that he had delivered for Señor Galdame; one hand with a coin in it, for the reward that Pollito's work had won for him.

Marco shook his head to clear his vision. He looked at his own hands. One empty hand, covered in mud and bits of straw, for the work of building the colony. The other was empty too. No coin. Only more mud. What had Marco won for his work? Once, for a moment, there had been a pouch of gold around his neck. It was gone now—back on Matanza's belt. He had found the father he longed for. But his father, he was sure, saw him as a child and a crook. Now, like Juanita said, Marco played in the mud.

"And you what?" The voice shook Marco from his thoughts.

"What?"

"You do the work, and you what?" said Juanita again.

"Nothing," said Marco. He lowered his head, and packed mud into the next wooden frame. When he looked up, Juanita had disappeared.

"Wonderful," he said. "Now I have to pack the molds and move the frames myself." He was silent for the rest of the day. When he finally trudged away from his work, he left behind 327 adobe bricks.

———

Marco woke up late the next morning. The new colony was already ringing with the noises of morning work. Men whistled at horses, pounded with mallets, and strained to pull up roots and stones. Marco stumbled out of the adobe hut where he and his father lived. He couldn't see his father. Garrido carried a bundle of firewood toward the smithy. Marco shouted to him.

"Aye, Garrido!"

"Aye, Señor Polo! Look at you, all awake and it not even noon yet!" He laughed, and then continued. "Your father had hoped to greet you this morning, before he left."

"Left? Where is he?" asked Marco.

"Juan Ponce took some of the soldiers and went to read the Requirement to the natives," said Garrido.

"My father is not a soldier," said Marco, following Garrido to the smithy.

Garrido shrugged. "So he took some men that were not soldiers," he said. "Alonso is with them too. So is the priest. They will be back soon."

"Yes, the Requirement." asked Marco. "I've hoped to ask—what is a Requirement?"

"The Requirement is a long letter written by King Charles," said Garrido. "Juan Ponce is under the king's orders to read it to the natives." Garrido dropped the bundle of wood. "Juan Ponce is under orders, or he would not read it."

"Why wouldn't he read it? What does it say?"

"The Requirement?" asked Garrido. "The Requirement explains that the Pope is the voice of God in the world, just like St. Peter was so many years ago, and that the King is the voice of the Pope. And if the natives would please God, they should allow themselves to be governed by the King."

"And if they refuse?" asked Marco.

"Refuse they will, even if they can understand the letter, which isn't likely. It's in Castilian, after all. In any case, if they refuse, Juan Ponce is under orders to read it to them again."

"And if they refuse again?" asked Marco.

"Then everyone flashes their swords and fires their guns, and many natives are killed and many more are made slaves," answered Garrido.

"Hmm," said Marco.

Garrido answered, "Juan Ponce agrees with your 'hmm.' I do not know what arrangement Juan Ponce has made with the natives, but it has kept us safe for four months. It is not like the natives to leave us alone for so long. And now the Requirement. It is the priest, I think, that has convinced him to read it now. It has taken Juan Ponce four months to feel as if the natives are ready to hear it, and it gives him no pleasure even now to take it to them. We will see how much peace is left after today."

It was a serious day, Marco knew. Still, he could not help chuckling as he imagined the natives struggling to understand the letter. Marco wished Garrido well, and walked over to the rows of adobe.

He thought of Alonso—poor Alonso, who had come to

La Florida to be young again, and who savored every drop of every ladleful of water he was offered—savored it in hope. And today, Alonso was with Juan Ponce in the forest somewhere; not in a quest for the Fountain, but on an errand to read a silly letter from a silly king to natives who perhaps even now were scratching their heads and shrugging their shoulders. Marco wondered if kind, old Alonso would be made to lead Indians away on a rope as slaves. It was difficult to see in his mind. Marco imagined the disappointment of his friend—in search of magic water, and made instead to fight with natives.

Marco thought of his father. His father loved him, he knew. But he imagined disappointment in his father's eyes each time he looked at him. If only Marco could do some great thing here in the colony. If only he could prove that he was not just a boy. The New World had filled Marco with a longing to be more than he was—and for his father to see it. *Someday*, Marco thought, *someone will find the Fountain. Perhaps it will be me.*

Such were Marco's thoughts as he walked from his hut to the rows of adobe frames, waiting to be filled. Even from a distance, he could see that the oldest bricks—the ones that had been drying in the sun for days—were gone. Carted away this morning to make the walls of more buildings.

Juanita was waiting for him, sipping from a spoon

dipped in a bucket of water.

"So, the water has already come around?" asked Marco.

"This is my own water," said Juanita. "I brought it here myself. You may have some." She handed Marco the spoon.

Marco dipped the spoon into the bucket and took a cool drink.

"What is this?" he asked.

"It's water, idiot," said Juanita. "It tastes like something else?"

"Sweet. It's sweet," said Marco. "I've never tasted water like ... "

Marco lost himself in thought. Where was Alonso? There was something different about the water in Juanita's bucket. Marco began to get excited. *Someday, someone will find the Fountain,* he thought again. *And perhaps it will be me.*

"Juanita ... er ... Pedrito," he said. "Can you show me where you found this water?"

"Why should I," said Juanita.

The sweetness of the water lingered in Marco's mouth. He didn't know much about water, but something about the ladle full of water from Juanita's bucket prickled the hair on his neck. There was no reason for Juanita to break from her work and lead Marco to where she had found the water. There would surely be trouble if the children deserted their tasks, even for a little while. But Marco knew how to get what he wanted from Juanita. He had been holding one card all the way from San Juan. He played his card now.

"You'll show me the water, because if you don't, I'll tell the crew that you're a girl."

"No one would believe you!"

Marco shrugged. "It would not be difficult to prove," he said. "Now, where did this water come from?"

"I will show you," said Juanita.

"Let's go," said Marco. "And bring the bucket."

"Bring the bucket yourself," said Juanita. Marco did.

Juanita tramped away from the clearing, and into the woods. Tall and tangled trees rose up from a ground cover of squat palmettos. Soon, the noise of the colony died completely. Juanita walked some steps ahead of Marco, and to his left.

"How long have you known about this wa ... " said Marco. He stopped abruptly.

"What is it?" asked Juanita.

"Nothing," said Marco.

But it wasn't nothing. Between two great trees hung a monstrous spider web, as large as the topsail on the *Leonor*. Marco stood just inches from a great golden Orb Weaver, its legs long, black, and cruel. It was level with Marco's eyeballs.

In *La Florida*, it was impossible to go very far without discovering such a spider and its shining web. In the forests, they hung every few dozen yards. In the weeks since their landing, Marco had run headlong into more than one of them. Each encounter had left him thrashing and howling, slapping at his clothes to knock a giant spider from his body. No spider had ever injured him, but he had never gotten used to these natives of *La Florida*.

Marco's heart was in his throat even now. But the great spider did not move, and Marco had stopped shy of its web. Marco caught his breath, and stepped carefully out around the trees that held the web. He walked gingerly to where Juanita stood.

"Come on, we're almost there," said Juanita.

Marco followed Juanita, his eyes now focused not on the trees, but on the air between them, looking for webs. It gave him a headache, and as such, Marco didn't see the water until he had stepped into it.

"Very nice," said Juanita.

Marco's foot had stepped into soft, marshy mud. "This is the water I drank?" He felt ill.

"No, idiot. Was the bucket I gave you full of mud? Further up this way. Come on."

Skirting the mud, Juanita led Marco along a wide swath of marshy soil. It became wetter and wetter, and before long, clear, still water stood above the muck.

"We're getting close. Yes, there it is!" said Juanita. She pointed. Marco could hear water bubbling. Then he saw it— a gentle spring, where water rippled up from the ground beneath the rich foliage. Marco stared. The air was full of silence and mystery.

"How did you happen to find this place?" asked Marco.

"I found it yesterday. You called me lazy, and I didn't want to work with you anymore. I came exploring."

"And left me with all the work," Marco said.

"For a change," retorted Juanita. "Besides, I found this spring, and when we tell Juan Ponce, he'll be glad of our discovery, and maybe he'll trust us to go on more adventures instead of just packing adobe frames every day."

"I think he may be even more pleased than you know," said Marco.

"What do you mean?"

"I don't know why I think this—just a hunch on tasting the water from your bucket. But I think you may have found the Fountain."

"The Fountain? The fountain of magic water? The water that can make you young? Matanza says it's a myth," said Juanita. "He says that no one is even looking for the magic fountain."

"I know what Matanza says, and Matanza is an idiot,"

said Marco. "You've seen Alonso taste every drop of water he ever gets—as if he's waiting for some change. The Fountain is the secret dream of every man on this voyage, and you know it."

"The secret dream of every ten-year old boy on this voyage, you mean," said Juanita.

Marco looked at Juanita, hurt. He opened his mouth to try to explain why he knew this was the Fountain. But he had no words for it.

"Come on," he said. "Let's fill the bucket, and get back."

Marco and Juanita were silent as they made their way to the headwaters of the spring. Marco immersed the bucket, and began to draw it up again. Suddenly, he stopped. Juanita had placed a hand on his shoulder.

"What?"

"Shh."

Marco looked at Juanita. She was pointing into the trees beyond the spring. Marco followed with his eyes.

In the shade beneath the trees stood a man. His chest and legs were bare. His hair was gathered in a knot on top of his head. In one hand, he held what looked like a short spear—in the other, a smooth stick of wood with a hollowed-out place at one end. Around his neck were leather cords, strung with shells. He did not move, but his arms and legs were poised, as if at a word he could burst into a full run.

"He is Calusa?" whispered Juanita.

"I figure," said Marco.

"The ones that attacked Juan Ponce years ago?"

Marco did not answer. Juanita's grip on his shoulder grew tighter. Marco looked at Juanita's other hand. It held a rock the size of her fist.

"Don't do anything," whispered Marco.

"Do you know what the Calusa would do to a girl?" whispered Juanita.

"No."

"Me neither."

"Put the rock down, Juanita. No one knows you're a girl anyway."

Marco and Juanita were still bent over the spring, their eyes on the man in the trees. The man in the trees never moved his eyes. Neither did the children. A long time, it seemed, they stood, hearts pounding.

"What do you think he wants?" whispered Juanita.

"I don't know," said Marco slowly. "Maybe they guard the spring."

"I'm scared, Marco."

"Me too. Put down the rock."

At that moment, the man in the trees took a step

toward them. The movement startled them. Marco yelped. The yelp startled the man, and his spear arm raised on its own. Juanita screamed.

"No, Juanita, don't!"

Marco's cry came too late. Juanita let go of his shoulder, and hurled the rock with all her might. It spun in the air as it crossed the space between the children and the man. It struck the man on the side of the head. The man stumbled. Blood began to show on his temple. He made an exclamation that Marco did not understand.

From behind him in the trees, another Calusa man came.

"Run!" shouted Marco. He spun Juanita away from the two men, and the children burst away like birds through the forest. Behind them the two Calusa ran.

Palmettos sliced at Marco's legs as he ran through them. He could hear the men behind them, closing the distance. On they sped, flailing through brambly woods for the clearing where the colony lay. Calusa footfalls were deafening behind them.

"Look out!" Marco pushed Juanita out of the way of a giant web. Juanita stumbled as she changed trajectory, but did not fall. The Calusa behind them was not so lucky. Behind them, they heard what must have been a curse. Marco allowed himself a look. The man had plowed straight through the great web, and paused in a panic to swipe at the strands that clung to him, and to brush the huge spider from his body. The Calusa with the injured head ran past him, hot in pursuit of the children. In a moment, both men had resumed the chase. Marco and Juanita were both howling now, yelling in fear and confusion. They still could not see the colony beyond the forest.

Suddenly, Marco heard the snap of a string, and a sharp intake of breath. He craned his neck as he ran. The rear Calusa had fallen to the forest floor. He writhed on the ground with a crossbow bolt in his chest. In a moment he was still. From behind a stand of trees, someone ran out swiftly to meet them. The person held a crossbow in his arm. As he met the Calusa, the newcomer swung the weapon at his head. The Calusa wheeled to the ground from the blow. As soon as he hit the forest floor, he struggled again to rise. The newcomer was on him in an instant. He tackled the stunned Calusa, pinning his arm behind his back and pushing him to the ground on his stomach. He put his knee into the Calusa's spine, and held a crossbow bolt against the man's neck, hard, so the man could feel the sharp point. The Calusa went still. With one hand, the newcomer took a knife from his belt, and cut the cords from the Calusa's neck. He put the knife back in his belt, and with his teeth stripped the shells from the cords. Then he used the cords to tie the Calusa's hands. With his knee still in the Calusa's back, he loaded a bolt into the crossbow. Finally, he turned to face the children. Marco's eyes went wide.

The newcomer was Matanza.

"Why did you leave the colony?" scolded Matanza.

The children were too frightened to speak.

"Why?" shouted Matanza.

Matanza's shout startled Juanita into speech.

"Marco thought we'd found the Fou—"

"There was something we wanted to bring to Juan Ponce," Marco interrupted.

"Whatever it was, we will bring him something better," said Matanza. "His first slave in *La Florida*. Here."

Matanza handed something to Marco. It was the Calusa's short spear, and the shaft with the cup on the end. Marco didn't know what to do with them.

"Just carry them back to the colony," said Matanza.

The Calusa was conscious, and Matanza dragged him to his feet. There was dirt on his chest and on his face. Blood flowed from the place where Juanita's rock had hit him, and from where Matanza had struck him with the crossbow. Marco looked at the man's face. It was difficult to read what was written there. Marco felt sure that if

Matanza had not come, he and Juanita would both have come to harm. But Marco also wondered what might have happened if Juanita had not thrown the rock.

It was useless to think about. Juanita had thrown the rock. Now, leaving the dead man in the forest, Matanza pushed the wounded Calusa in front of him. The children followed silently behind.

Before long, the trees thinned, and the silent group walked into the clearing where the buildings of the colony stood.

Marco blinked at what he saw.

Juan Ponce stood with his back to them. With him were a handful of soldiers, Alonso, Marco's father, and other colonists who had gathered to watch. Across from Juan Ponce stood a group of Calusa. Some held weapons in their hands. Juan Ponce and his company had brought the Calusa to the colony—to see it and to hear the Requirement. Juan Ponce held a great scroll before him, and read in a loud voice:

...and that you acknowledge the Church as the Ruler and Superior of the whole world, and the high priest called Pope, and in his name the King and Queen as superiors and lords and kings of these islands and this mainland ...

The words went on. Marco didn't understand a word that he heard—something about Charles being king of the land where the natives lived.

But Juan Ponce did not finish reading the letter. At that moment, one of the Calusa saw Marco and the others coming into the clearing. He whispered to his companions. In an instant, they were all looking at Matanza and the man that he pushed before him. Matanza saw what was going on, and tried to push the captive behind a building as they passed. But it was too late. The Calusa men around Juan Ponce had seen him—had seen the cords that tied his hands and had seen the blood on his face and head. The men broke into a frenzy of talk and pointing. One of them shouted loudly into the face of Juan Ponce. Soldiers went for their swords. Calusa raised their spears. Juan Ponce held up his hands, as if to calm the crowd. Amid the shouting, three of the Calusa ran toward where Matanza stood with his prisoner. Matanza pushed his prisoner to his knees. Then he raised the crossbow at one of his attackers, and released the bolt. One of the Calusa fell. Another reached Matanza before he could reload. The Calusa raised a heavy club, and brought it down on Matanza's head. Matanza fell like a stone. The Calusa bent to cut the cords around the hands of Matanza's prisoner. The third Calusa moved in the direction of the children.

Marco's father ran toward them, and screamed as he ran. "*Oh, Dios!* Marco! Run!" Marco dropped the spear and the shaft he carried, and he and Juanita darted through an open doorway. Marco slammed the wooden door and threw his weight against it. The weight of the Calusa's body drove into the door from the outside. Marco yelped, and pushed harder against the door. But the Calusa did not pound again. Marco heard his father reach the Indian. There was a sound of fists on flesh. Marco opened the door. The Calusa lay on the ground, unconscious. The clearing where the colony stood was a confusion of running and shouting. Colonists ran to barricade themselves inside huts. Soldiers struggled to load crossbows and draw swords. Some scrambled for metal tools or heavy sticks to use as weapons. Marco's father had drawn a knife. He was running away from Marco's shelter—into the confusion. He shouted back at Marco.

"Close the door, Marco! Do not open it again!"

But Marco could not tear his eyes from the scene. He stood with the door open.

"Close the door, Marco!" Juanita screamed behind him. Marco did not move. He watched as his father ran across the clearing, toward a Calusa warrior. Marco could see the blood on the warrior's face from where Juanita had hit him with a rock. It was Matanza's prisoner. But the warrior did not see Marco's father. He was looking somewhere else. In a split second, as Marco watched, the warrior scooped up what Marco had let fall as he ran. He fitted the butt of the long dart into the cupped end of the shaft. The warrior lifted the shaft, and held it behind his head. As Marco's father reached him, the warrior flicked the shaft forward. Like a bolt of lightning, the spear left the shaft and sped across the clearing. Marco followed it with his eyes—and gasped as it came to rest: in the thigh of Juan Ponce de Leon. The explorer slumped to the ground.

Marco's heart careened against his ribs. He glanced back at his father, who had taken the Calusa by surprise. The Calusa flailed against a few blows, and then turned and fled. Marco's father gave chase.

Marco scurried like a rabbit through the battle to where Juan Ponce had fallen. The thigh—where the dart had lodged—bled savagely. Juan Ponce, through glazed eyes, saw Marco. "Marco Polo, yes?" said Juan Ponce with a grimace. "You should go indoors."

Marco shrugged.

Juan Ponce looked at him for a moment. "Come then. Help me with this leg."

Marco did not hesitate. He grasped the dart with both hands, and pulled with all his might. Juan Ponce screamed. The dart remained in his leg. Marco felt sick.

Juan Ponce's eyes rolled backward. "Come now, Marco," he gasped. "There is a jagged tip on the end of the dart that will not pull backward so easily." Juan Ponce swallowed. "You must break the shaft of the dart in half, yes?"

"Yes," said Marco. His head began to swim, but he grasped the exposed dart in both hands. With a heave, he snapped it in two.

"Good," whispered Juan Ponce. "Now, listen. You must push the dart the rest of the way through my leg."

"What?" whispered Marco. His hands began to shake.

"Yes, Marco. Concentrate," said Juan Ponce between gasps. "You must push the dart through. When it breaks the skin, it will pull easily out the other side."

"I don't think I can ... " began Marco.

"Come, Marco Polo," said Juan Ponce. He looked right into Marco's eyes. "Help me with my leg, yes?"

Marco's breath came in shallow gasps. But he grasped the arrow with both hands. He pushed. Juan Ponce screamed. So did Marco. Juan Ponce leaned forward and put his hands on Marco's. Together, they pushed. In a moment, the head of the dart broke the skin on the backside of Juan Ponce's thigh. Juan Ponce reached for the shaft of the dart, and drew it out of his leg. He smiled weakly at Marco.

"To have a Marco on the voyage is a good omen, no?" he said. Then he let his head fall backward onto the ground.

Marco listened. The noise in the clearing had changed. No more sounds of battle—just a heavy silence, punctuated by the soft moans of the wounded and the comforting words of those who tended to them. Marco wondered how long he had taken with Juan Ponce's leg. He turned slowly around, and felt the blood flush in his face.

There stood his father. Alonso stood there too, and Garrido, holding Juanita by the hand. A few others had begun to attend to Juan Ponce.

Marco felt sheepish. "How long have you been standing there?" asked Marco, perplexed and exhausted.

"Long enough," said Marco's father quietly.

"You did not rush in to help me?" asked Marco.

"It was clear that Juan Ponce was in good hands," said Marco's father.

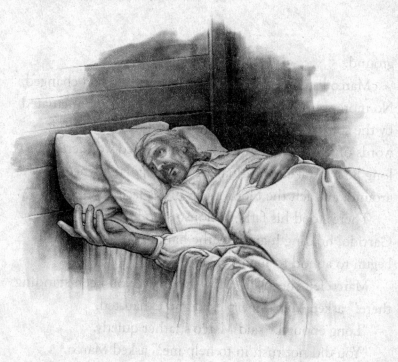

Chapter 11

Marco was not invited to the councils that decided the fate of the colony. In fact, he disappeared alone into the woods as the leaders of the colony met and thought. By the time he came back, the council had decided: The Calusa had been routed, but they would be back. Juan Ponce's leg was growing worse, and he could not be cared for in the colony. Others were dead. Many of the survivors were wounded. And so it was that Marco found himself on the beach, ready to board *La Fuente*. He held tightly to the handle of a bucket—the last thing to be loaded. Next to him stood Garrido.

"You will not come to Cuba, then?" asked Marco.

"No, I will not come to Cuba. Going to Cuba would not be a good trip. Coming to *La Florida*—this was not a good trip either. I go now on the *Leonor* to Veracruz, where Cortes changes the world. We will bring him some crossbows. We will bring him some powder for his cannons, and a few soldiers. Maybe he will be pleased. Maybe he will decide to pay us. Maybe it will be a good trip then. He is a famous man, no?"

"I will miss you, Garrido."

"I will miss you too, Señor."

"I hope you can change the world with Cortes," said Marco.

"Let us not talk of changing the world," said Garrido. "It will be enough to have a good trip, yes?"

After what seemed like only a few moments more, Marco stood on the deck of *La Fuente*. The hold was empty, but for the few supplies that they would need for the week-long voyage to Cuba. Marco's bucket had been carefully placed in a corner of the hold. On *La Florida*, in the center of the clearing where the empty colony stood, they left a handful of quiet graves. Matanza's was among them. Juan Ponce, injured as he was, had been luckier than some.

The cows and pigs, sheep and chickens had been let loose on *La Florida* ("When someone comes back here," Alonso had joked mournfully, "there will not be ten cows, but a hundred. It is kind of us, no?").

Marco, his father, Alonso, Juanita, and a handful of others sailed for Cuba on *La Fuente*. Half of those languished in the forecastle, wounded and delirious. Juan Ponce lay on his bed in the captain's cabin, sweating under a high fever. Garrido and the rest of the men, along with most of the horses, sailed aboard the *Leonor*, bound for Veracruz and Cortes—looking for the conquest and glory that had escaped them in *La Florida*.

For one day, the two ships sailed together. During that day, they buried a man at sea—Hernan Ponce ("He was my nephew, did you know?" said Juan Ponce. "What will I tell his family?"). Then the ships parted. A soft, warm rain fell as *La Fuente* veered east—the *Leonor*, west.

The winds were fair, and the ship plowed quietly toward Cuba. In addition to his other duties, Marco tended the sick—changing dressings on wounds, and bringing cool water to those too weak to fetch it themselves.

"May I see Juan Ponce?" Marco asked often.

The answer was the same, whether it came from his

father or from Alonso: "Juan Ponce must rest. Later you ask again, yes?"

Juan Ponce's fever worsened. Often, he slept. When he was awake, he would sometimes ask a crewman to read to him from the Bible. Sometimes it was Alonso's turn. Sometimes it was Marco's father's turn. Marco's father was not a good reader. He was slow, and halted over words. Reading to Juan Ponce exhausted him. Still, when he was called, he read; he read until he was asked to stop, or until Juan Ponce was asleep.

On the evening of the second day, Marco watched as his father came from Juan Ponce's cabin.

"Is Don Juan awake?" Marco asked.

"He is awake, and resting," said Marco's father.

Marco paused. Then he spoke. "I would like to see him."

Marco's father looked at Marco. The boy had fetched the bucket from the corner of the hold. "He is not well, son."

"I know. If he will see me, I would like to see him."

"If he attends you now, you will stop asking?"

Marco nodded.

Marco's father turned back to the door of Juan Ponce's cabin. He opened it, and disappeared for a moment. Then he was back. "Don Juan says that he would be happy to see you."

"Thank you, Father. Forgive me." Marco stepped past his father, and into the cabin of Juan Ponce de Leon.

A single lantern lit the cabin. In its yellow glow, Marco saw Juan Ponce. He lay in bed, his white shirt open at the collar, and a sheet pulled tight around his chest. The sheet covered him, but had been pulled back from his injured leg, which rested, dressed, on a folded blanket. Beads of sweat stood on the explorer's forehead. His pale hands rested above the sheet. When he saw Marco, he reached a hand in the boy's direction.

"Marco Polo," he said, weakly. A smile spread itself thinly over his face.

"Forgive me for disturbing you, Señor," said Marco.

"It is no trouble to be attended ... " Juan Ponce took a deep breath, "by the boy who saved my life."

Marco was silent for a moment. Then he spoke again.

"I hope that you are thirsty, Señor. I have something that I would like you to drink."

"Drink?"

"Sì, Señor. It is from *La Florida*. Pedrito found a spring. The night of the attack I went back. I was frightened, but I went back and brought aboard this bucket of water from the fountain that we found. This is the first moment that I've been allowed to come to you." Marco's voice lowered.

"I think it was *the* Fountain," he whispered.

"*The* Fountain? Of which fountain do you speak?"

Marco could not believe his ears. Perhaps he wasn't explaining himself clearly enough. "The fountain of water to make a man forever young," said Marco.

For a moment, Juan Ponce was silent. Then, his shoulders began to shake. Marco grew worried. Juan Ponce began to gasp. Marco stepped to his side. But Juan Ponce was not gasping in pain. His shoulders were not convulsing with fever. Juan Ponce was laughing.

"Señor?" asked Marco.

"*The* Fountain." Juan Ponce's face cracked in a wide smile. "I remember. Ferdinand—do you remember King Ferdinand?"

"I never met the king," said Marco.

"Pity. Ferdinand was always so convinced of the Fountain—right up until the end; the legends, you know. He was glad of the gold and the crops on San Juan, but he always hoped that I would discover the Fountain. Poor, dear fool. Poor, dear, dead fool."

"Fool?" said Marco.

Juan Ponce spoke slowly, his hand outstretched toward Marco. "It would be easy to sit on a throne made of gold and think that a magical fountain of youth is the most wonderful thing in the world, yes? But you and I know better."

"You and I?" Marco was confused.

"We, who have traveled the world, and seen things lovelier than youth—and more terrifying than growing old."

"I do not understand," said Marco. "What do we know?"

"What do we know? We know that one might pour a hundred gallons of magic water down the throat of a king on a throne and he will still be old—but let an old man walk on the soil of the New World for one day and he will live forever."

"So the magic is in the soil and not the water?" asked Marco.

Juan Ponce began to laugh again. "The magic is neither in the soil, nor in the water, Marco." Juan Ponce paused. "It is in the getting up off of one's fat throne. It is ... it is in the going."

"But I thought the Fountain was—"

"For this you come to the New World?" interrupted Juan Ponce. "For magical water?"

"I came to the New World because I was hit on the head by pirates," said Marco, sheepishly.

"Indeed," said Juan Ponce. "But I did not ask *by* what you came into the New World. I asked *for* what you came."

"I do not understand," said Marco.

"You, Alonso, your other friend Garrido, and the other, who was killed in the attack ... "

"Matanza," said Marco.

"Yes, Matanza. You all came here by the same means—by way of a supply ship, *La Juana*, yes? Is this right? Did I hear right?"

"Yes, it is true, we came aboard *La Juana*."

"So you all came *by* the same means, yes? But what did you come *for*?"

Marco was still confused.

Juan Ponce slowly licked his lips. His voice grew weaker from moment to moment. But he continued. "Matanza is like Cortes. He came for gold and for slaves. Matanza died under the same rules by which he lived. Perhaps Cortes will meet the same fate. Garrido, he comes for nothing more than to be paid for honest work—perhaps he will find it as well with Cortes as with me. Poor, good Alonso, he comes for magic water to make him young—perhaps he will never find it. But is there a man on this voyage as young as he?"

Marco smiled.

Juan Ponce spoke again. "It is not often ours to choose *how* we come to the crossroads. But it is always ours to choose what we come *for*. You are a child in the New World, Marco. What an adventure it will be—learning for what you have come. The adventure is more fountain than the Fountain could ever be."

Marco was silent. He did not know what to say. "I will let you rest now, Don Juan."

"Thank you, Marco Polo."

Marco turned toward the cabin door. He reached for the latch. Juan Ponce stopped him.

"Marco, when your father was a child, the world was only half the size it is now. Señor Columbus, in three small ships, set foot on Hispaniola, and the world grew. I set foot on *La Florida*, and it grew again. The world is now twice the size as when your father was a child, and we who made it grow will be forever on the lips of those who speak of the New World—forever young. See what the tiny feet of a few tiny men can do? You will remember this, yes?"

"I will remember." Marco turned again toward the door. Again, Juan Ponce stopped him.

"What made you believe your spring to be the magic fountain?"

"It tasted sweet, Señor. It tasted sweet and I was thinking of the Fountain as I drank from Pedrito's bucket. I suppose that's all."

"Sulfur water, probably," said Juan Ponce, with a thin smile. "Will you kindly throw the rest over the side?"

"Yes, Don Juan," said Marco.

"And Boy?"

"Yes?"

"To have a Marco on the voyage is a good omen, no?"

Marco didn't answer. But it didn't matter. Juan Ponce had fallen asleep.

Chapter 12

The gangway of *La Fuente* was down, and Marco's father helped Alonso and the others load the wounded onto the dock and into wagons. Marco gathered the few belongings that he and his father owned, and stowed them in his father's sea bag. Finished with the wounded, his father climbed the gangplank. They stood at the rail together, Marco and his father, looking out to sea.

"Will Juan Ponce live?" asked Marco.

"His fever has not broken. I have no way with wounded, but I fear the worst."

There was silence between them.

Juanita emerged from the forecastle. "There are no more wounded in there," she said. "I will follow the wagons and explain what happened, if I can. Good-bye Marco."

"Good-bye, Pedrito," said Marco. Juanita ran down the gangplank in the direction of the wagons. Marco's father called after her.

"*Ai*, Pedrito!" Juanita turned.

"Be a good girl, now, yes?" Juanita stiffened, and her face went white.

Marco's father grinned. Juanita grinned back. Then she turned and ran out of sight.

"You knew?" said Marco.

"Who did not know?" said Marco's father. He shrugged. "She was very earnest, but it is difficult to pretend for very long."

Father and son laughed together. "Will she be alright?"

Marco's father raised his eyebrows. "It is difficult to say, but when she gets to where the wounded are, she will find Alonso, who has a good reputation for helping children find their way, no? Speaking of which ... " Marco's father reached into his shirt and withdrew something that Marco recognized. It was Matanza's pouch—still heavy with gold coins. "I meant no dishonor to Matanza's name to take this before he was buried," he said. "Had Matanza earned it, I would never have touched it. But as you know, he was part of a curious triangle of thieves. Only one of them remains here now to claim it. I thought you might know best what to do with this." He placed the pouch on the rail next to Marco.

Marco looked at the pouch, then spoke. "Then you still see me as a thief?"

"When I look at you," said his father, "I see sturdy buildings on *La Florida*. I see an arrow pulled from a wounded man's leg while battle rages around. I see kindness enough to keep the secret of a companion, though she may not deserve it. I see a ready nurse to the wounded. I see courage enough to sneak back to a spring in the midst of enemies to bring healing to a friend. I care not what we face from here. I am in the ablest of company. I am proud to have you as my son. And it is enough."

There was a moment's hesitation. A half-second in which Marco's imagination fought his impulse. Then, quick as a cricket, he lifted the pouch lightly in his palm, and threw it far out into the sea.

Marco's father watched calmly as the pouch broke the surface of the water, and disappeared beneath it. "There was great fortune in that pouch," he said.

"I think the greater fortune lies in being free of it," said Marco.

Marco's father pulled Marco to him. He lifted Marco to his hip. The boy held to his father's neck. Marco's father flung his sea bag over his shoulder, and together they descended the gangway.

The wharf in Cuba was much like the wharf in San Juan, or in Spain. The ocean seemed just as vast from here as from anywhere else. It was as if Marco had come again to a beginning in the New World. And for what had he come? Marco couldn't wait to find out.

Author's Note

When Christopher Columbus sailed in 1493 (on his second trip to the New World), among his crew was a young knight named Juan Ponce de Leon. A year earlier, Juan Ponce had fought in the battle of Granada- the battle that drove the last of the Moors from Spain (winning that battle gave the King and Queen of Spain a little breathing room, after years of war—enough breathing room to finally lend an ear to Columbus, and to support his voyage of discovery).

Juan Ponce was young when Columbus brought him on the voyage of 1493, and for most of the rest of his life, he made his home in the New World. People who knew him might have described him as a farmer, a businessman, a colonist, or a warrior-and they would all have been right. Juan Ponce planted crops, oversaw mining operations, governed the Spanish settlement on San Juan, and subdued Caribbean natives.

In 1513—twenty years after sailing to the New World with Columbus— Juan Ponce made his own voyage of discovery. On that voyage, he became the first European—as far as we know—to set foot on Florida soil (he called it La Pascua Florida—"the flowery easter"—La Florida for short). But there was more: he also discovered the Gulf Stream-a mighty ocean current that moves warm water from the straits of Florida all the way to Newfoundland. Riding the Gulf Stream, ships could travel from the New World to Europe faster than anyone had imagined. Such discoveries made the New World a more exciting place than ever before, and made Juan Ponce a famous man.

Following that voyage, Juan Ponce spent eight years hoping to go back to Florida–this time, to establish a permanent colony. And if he dreamed of glory and immortality through more adventures, he wasn't alone; others had their eyes on the New World as well. In 1519, Hernan Cortes sailed to colonize Mexico, and captured the world's attention with one of the most dramatic conquests in history.

Finally, in 1521, Juan Ponce's chance came. Permission for a new voyage had been obtained from the crown. Other men led the colony in San Juan. Juan Ponce's children were grown and married. The time was right, and for Juan Ponce, it was to be his greatest voyage yet.

This book is an imagined account of that voyage, and the story of how a boy like Marco might have become a part of it. Marco, Matanza, and Juanita are fictional characters. Alonso de Jerèz, Juan Garrido, and Pedro Jimenez are mostly imagined, though their names come from actual passengers aboard Juan Ponce's voyage.

If you enjoyed this book and would like to know more about Juan Ponce, there are some books you might look for. For a good, easy read, try Gail Sakurai's "Juan Ponce de Leòn." I also found myself very thankful to Robert H. Fuson's "Juan Ponce de Leòn and the Spanish Discovery of Puerto Rico and Florida." I also had fun reading about Juan Ponce's voyage of 1513 in a book called "Ponce de Leòn and the Discovery of Florida" by Douglas Peck, who retraced Juan Ponce's voyage all by himself in a yacht called "Gooney Bird."

"Marco and the Fountain of Youth" is just the beginning. I hope you'll join me for the rest of the Florida Adventure Series.